THE CASTLE OF OTRANTO

DOVER THRIFT EDITIONS

Horace Walpole

DOVER PUBLICATIONS, INC.
MINEOLA, NEW YORK

DOVER THRIFT EDITIONS

GENERAL EDITOR: PAUL NEGRI

Bibliographical Note

This Dover edition, first published in 2004, is an unabridged republication of *The Castle of Otranto* (Second Edition) including two prefaces and the editor's introduction; and Sir Walter Scott's *Introduction* to *The Castle of Otranto*, as first published by Ballantyne, Edinburgh, 1811; all from *Three Gothic Novels*, edited by E. F. Bleiler, originally published by Dover Publications, Inc., New York, 1966.

Library of Congress Cataloging-in-Publication Data

Walpole, Horace, 1717–1797.
　　The Castle of Otranto / Horace Walpole.
　　　　p. cm.
　　ISBN-13: 978-0-486-43412-4
　　ISBN-10: 0-486-43412-5
　　　1. Inheritance and succession—Fiction. 2. Castles—Fiction. 3. Italy—Fiction. I. Title.

PR3757.W2C3 2004
823'.6—dc22

2003070015

Manufactured in the United States by LSC Communications
43412506　　2017
www.doverpublications.com

Contents

INTRODUCTION

Horace Walpole and
The Castle of Otranto

During much of the first half of the eighteenth century England was ruled by Sir Robert Walpole, later Lord Orford, one of the most successful rough-and-tumble politicians of the time. His son Horace (1717–1797) did not share his fierce energy, but was a gentle, sickly, somewhat effeminate boy. Indeed, one of the speculations several generations later was that Horace Walpole was not the son of Sir Robert, but of a friend of the family, Carr, Lord Hervey. This scandal is not taken too seriously nowadays, but it points up the strong concern in Walpole's two major works of fiction with questions of paternity.

His youth was uneventful. He spent three years at Cambridge University with the poets Thomas Gray and William Mason, who were his close friends, but left without a degree. In 1739, accompanied by Gray, he set out on the Grand Tour of France and Italy, and returned in 1741. He had been intended for the law and politics, but he showed no aptitude for legal matters, and after a brief attempt at a political career, he wisely limited himself to sitting occasionally in Parliament. But even after his father's death he had powerful connections among the Whigs, and he occasionally tried his hand at pamphleteering and small scale behind-the-scenes manipulations.

Sir Robert Walpole, although not a man of great fortune, had left Horace a good income, and when this was combined with the salary from various political sinecures which Horace held most of his life, he hovered in a reasonably satisfactory financial milieu. He was neither poor, like his friend Gray, nor fantastically wealthy like the later William Beckford. He could satisfy most of his wants, as long as they remained within reason, and yet was in no danger of becoming jaded with acquisition.

Walpole became primarily a man of society. He made friends easily, and he was an indefatigable enthusiast, perpetually ferreting about contagiously among antiquities of various sorts. Since he had little else to do and his acquaintance numbered many people of much the same intellect, temperament and circumstances as himself, he corresponded voluminously. One of the glories of English literature is the enormous corpus of thousands of letters that he wrote to his many friends in both England and France.

Several pictures survive of Horace Walpole in his early maturity, and they show him a man well suited to the correspondence. He was a handsome man, very reminiscent in physical feature and expression of some of the more ineffectual roles played by the modern actor Sir Alec Guinness: an air of refinement, whimsicality, intelligence, slightly chagrined embarrassment, zest, and a slight touch of malice.

In 1749 Horace Walpole began his unique contribution to European culture by buying Strawberry Hill, a small farm with a broad view of the Thames, on a main road near Twickenham, not far from London. He had rented the property for two years earlier. What he first intended to do with Strawberry Hill, beyond using it as a summer residence, we do not know, although apparently he toyed with the idea of building in various picturesque architectural styles. By late 1749 or early 1750, however, he had come to a decision: he would enlarge the cottage on the property and turn it into a "castellino" in the English Gothic style. He wrote to his friend Sir Horace Mann, who was in the diplomatic service in Florence, and requested whatever "Gothic fragments" (by which he meant medieval artifacts) could be found cheaply. He also took counsel with his friends Bentley, Chute and (later) Gray, as to what should be done.

One difficulty in creating the new Strawberry Hill was that Walpole was neither an architect nor an antiquary (although he later became skilled in antiquities), and a somewhat nebulous "taste" had to function in creating the castle. He seems never to have realized that Gothic was an art of construction, and not simply a decoration, and his interpretation of the form was peculiarly limited to surfaces and visibilities. He could not afford groining or fretwork for the stairways, but he felt they were necessary. According to his practice he might have made them out of plaster and lath; he might have made them out of carved cardboard; but what he actually did was simply paste up wallpaper with groining painted on it. For battlements he nailed cardboard on the framework of the cottage. One of the quips of the day was that Horrie had outlived four sets of battlements.

The work on Strawberry Hill progressed slowly, for Walpole was forced to live and to build upon his income. Perpetually in building, the castle grew from a small cottage into a long sprawling concatenation of rooms, about each of which Walpole became enthusiastic as it took form. The library and refectory were added in 1754; the gallery, round tower, great cloister and cabinet by 1760 and 1761; the north bedchamber in 1770. The guiding principle for the edifice was imitation of whatever building or architectural feature Walpole and his friends happened to like at the moment. The result, even though Walpole and his friends grew in antiquarian knowledge, was an architectural monstrosity, but apparently a monstrosity with charm, since it represented the interests, enthusiasms and achievements of an intelligent, gracious man.

Walpole tried to furnish his castle appropriately—that is, with a mixture of period pieces and quaint oddities which conveyed the mood of Gothicness to him. He imported stained glass windows showing saints in various torments or benedictions. He stuffed "niches full of trophies of old coats of mail, Indian shields made of rhinoceros hide, broadswords, quivers, longbows—all supposed to be taken by Sir Terry Robsart [a humorously invented apocryphal ancestor] in the Holy Wars." He also started a library and art collection, both characterized by the same whimsy, taste, intelligence and resourcefulness. Walpole was never a profound scholar or a true bibliophile, but his collection was nevertheless remarkable.

The significance of Strawberry Hill and its furnishings is that it marks the first important occasion that anyone had waxed enthusiastic over the life and artifacts of the Middle Ages. Before Walpole (apart from Bishop Hurd's less important *Letters on Chivalry*) the word "gothick" was almost always a synonym for rudeness, barbarousness, crudity, coarseness and lack of taste. After Walpole the word assumed two new major meanings: first, vigorous, bold, heroic and ancient, and second, quaint, charming, romantic, perhaps a little decadent in its association with Romanism, but sentimental and interesting.

Strawberry Hill rapidly became one of the showplaces of England, all the more so because of Walpole's political and cultural connections, and visitors from all over England, even from the Continent, were to write Walpole for permission to visit and admire it. Walpole graciously set aside certain days for tours through his creation. It became the symbol of a new aesthetic experience, and to Walpole, after a time, it became more than just a dwelling and a fanciful hobby. It may well have assumed the status of a macrocosm of himself. Just as William Beckford's Fonthill became interlinked with the personality of its builder and owner, Strawberry Hill became Horace Walpole— so much so that it formed a new image of itself in his novel *The Castle of Otranto*.

A project that Walpole had long fancied was the establishment of a printing press, from which he could issue whatever he felt worthy of preservation. In 1757 he founded the famous Strawberry Hill Press (Officina Arbuteana), beginning its existence with the publication of works by Gray. For thirty-two years the Press remained in existence, producing, as Wilmarth S. Lewis has stated, more lasting work, proportionately, than any other press in British history.

It is something of a surprise, therefore, to learn that Walpole's most important work, *The Castle of Otranto*, was not printed at Strawberry Hill, as is sometimes claimed, but was prepared commercially in London in a five-hundred-copy edition. Proclaimed to be a translation from the Italian text of Onufrio Muralto (which name is obviously reminiscent of Horace Walpole), it appeared on Christmas Eve, 1764. Walpole immediately sent out copies to his friends and to reviewers, displaying tactics common to pseudonymous authors: an eager desire to claim the credit if the work is praised, and an equally strong urge to disclaim responsibility if it is damned. As a result, many of Walpole's letters which mention *The Castle of Otranto* are very coy about it, and many of his acquaintances (who have been followed by some modern critics) considered the book to be an enormous, pointless joke.

Walpole's true attitude would seem to have been complex and not easily summarized. He was a whimsical man, and even when he was serious, he found it difficult to avoid flights of fancy. He was also a shy man, despite his gregariousness and social virtuosity, who could pretend an attitude of detached irony toward something about which he had strong feelings. While it is often said that *The Castle of Otranto* was a very elaborate spoof, because Walpole referred to it with diffidence and flippancy, it is much more likely that there is a solid center of sincerity within the story.

The origins of *The Castle of Otranto* are a confused welter of conscious and unconscious material. In Walpole's preface to the second edition of the novel, he declares that he wished to bridge a gap between the romances of old, which were all marvel and wonder, and the realistic novel of his own day, by which he probably meant the work of Richardson and Fielding. There is no reason to doubt this statement; it fits his novel reasonably well. But beyond this conscious literary attempt were other factors. Walpole, in his letter of March 9, 1765, wrote to Rev. William Cole:

> Your partiality to me and Strawberry have, I hope, inclined you to excuse the wildness of the story. You will even have found some traits to put you in mind of this place. When you read of the picture quitting its panel, did you not recollect the portrait of Lord Falkland, all in white, in my Gallery? Shall I even confess to you, what was the origin of this romance! I waked one morning, in the beginning of last June, from a dream, of which, all I could recover, was, that I had thought myself in an ancient castle (a very natural dream for a head like mine filled with Gothic story), and that on the uppermost banister of a great staircase I saw a gigantic hand in armour. In the evening I sat down, and began to write, without knowing in the least what I intended to say or relate. The work grew on my hands, and I grew fond of it. . . . In short, I was so engrossed with my Tale, which I completed in less than two months, that one evening, I wrote from the time I had drunk my tea, about six o'clock, till half an hour after one in the morning, when my hand and fingers were so weary, that I could not hold the pen to finish my sentence, but left Matilda and Isabella talking in the middle of a paragraph.

Strawberry Hill is the setting of Walpole's novel, and even small items of decoration are represented, as much as fictional necessities permit.

Elements of cryptamnesia also entered the novel. When parallels between the historical dukedom of Otranto and Walpole's novel were pointed out, Walpole denied the connection, even though references could be found among his books and there was no reason (if Walpole had remembered it) to deny it. Similarly, reminiscences of his old college at Cambridge were to be found in the castle of Otranto, as Walpole himself later recognized in a letter that is often overlooked:

> Two or three years later [after *The Castle of Otranto*] I went to the University of Cambridge, where I had passed three years of my youth. In entering one of the colleges, which I had entirely forgotten, I found myself exactly in the court of my Castle. The towers, the gates, the chapel, the great hall, everything answered with the greatest exactness. In fine, the idea of this college had remained in my head without my thinking of it and I had used it as the plan of my Castle without being conscious of it myself.

Walpole's life after the appearance of *The Castle of Otranto* was uneventful and continued the same patterns as had already been established. He went to Paris in 1765, was presented at the French court, and became entangled in the quarrel that broke out between Hume and Rousseau. He returned to England the following year, and continued his literary work. In 1768 he was approached by Chatterton, who sent copies of "Rowley" poems to him. Walpole submitted them to Gray and Mason, who declared them hoaxes, and Walpole rejected them. Chatterton committed suicide not long after this, and Walpole was unjustly condemned for not having helped him. Strawberry Hill continued to expand. The gout bothered Walpole more and more, and there are gruesome stories of calculi that emerged from sores on his knuckles and toes. Disabled most of the time and barely able to hobble around, he still remained the great epistolographer of his age, continuing his correspondence almost until his death. He inherited the title Lord Orford in 1791, when he was seventy-four, but was too old and feeble to sit in the House of Lords. He died in 1797.

ii

Horace Walpole was a very prolific writer if his many varied areas of activity are all taken into account. Much of his production was trivial, but his contemporaries considered several of his works important. These were (apart from *The Castle of Otranto*) his *Anecdotes of Painting in England,* a compilation of material about British artists, based on notes taken by George Vertue; *The Mysterious Mother,* a tragedy in blank verse; and *Historic Doubts on the Life and Reign of King Richard III,* which was the first attempt to prove Richard III innocent of murdering the two little princes. Today, however, Walpole is remembered for two achievements: the largest, most vivacious, most revealing body of letters in the English language, and his novel, *The Castle of Otranto.*

This novel has been called one of the half-dozen historically most important novels in English. The founder of a school of fiction, the so-called Gothic novel, it served as the direct model for an enormous quantity of novels written up through the first quarter of the nineteenth century; at one or more steps removed, it has inspired imitations and influenced other forms on up to the present. It was probably the most important source for enthusiasm for the Middle Ages that suddenly swept Europe in the later eighteenth century, and many of the trappings of the early nineteenth century Romantic movement have been traced to it. It embodied the spirit of an age. There are several full studies of the development of this Gothic spirit within the English novel and it is not necessary to provide a detailed recapitulation of it here, but it is always interesting to see how a concept becomes changed by transmission and how individuals wittingly or unwittingly manipulate an accepted form and mirror other conditions around them.

A generation or so often has to pass before awareness of a prototypical work can seep down to readers and writers of popular literature. Such was the case with the detective story form crystallized by Poe around 1841, which did not become a truly popular form until the 1880's and 1890's in the hands of Doyle, Richard Marsh, Fergus Hume, "Dick Donovan" and others. Such was also the case with the early science-fiction works of H. G. Wells (1895–1905); it took approximately thirty years before American science-fiction was able to use them as foundations. And such was the history of Walpole's *Castle of Otranto.* Appreciated at first only by a coterie of friends and fellow spirits of Walpole's, it received tempered praise in *The Monthly Review* and was damned by *The Critical Review.* It went into a second printing of five hundred copies in April 1765, and it was translated into French in 1767. Its first adaptation into a play—an important barometer of public taste during this period—occurred in 1781 at Covent Garden, where Robert Jephson, assisted by Walpole, dramatized the romance under the title of *The Count of Narbonne.* It was not especially successful, though it was later printed in a stand-ard collection of plays. Actually, it does not resemble *The Castle of Otranto* very much; all the supernaturalism has dropped out and only the disinheritance and alienation plot remains.

Imitation began very slowly. In 1777 Clara Reeve wrote in her preface to *The Champion of Virtue* (which is better known under its later title, *The Old English Baron*), "This story is the literary offspring of The Castle of Otranto." But not until the last decade of the eighteenth century was the influence of Walpole's romance felt strongly. Within this decade the Gothic novel achieved the status of a truly popular genre. Even the most superficial rela-tionship to Walpole's romance, the inclusion of the word "castle" in the title of a book, can be indicated for hundreds of novels found in this period. Some of these novels were long, and filled several volumes; others were small chapbooks issued to sell for sixpence, luridly illustrated with crude woodcuts.

Conventions were rigorously followed in the Gothic chain that followed Walpole's work. In most such novels the action takes place in the past, usually the Middle Ages, normally in and around a castle. Yet there is seldom any attempt to create verisimilitude or to build up antiquarian detail; in many cases the authors seem ignorant of the commonplaces of history. The Latin countries and Germany are most favored for a locale, although occasionally England is used. The supernatural is almost always present, although its nature and its quantity vary greatly from novel to novel. On the whole, the earlier novels used supernatural effects very sparingly, and as often as not explained those effects away at the end. The ghost might be a hermit who wants solitude; it might be a trick of coiners or bandits to keep away unwanted visitors; or it might simply be chance illusion. In all the novels of Ann Radcliffe, for example, there is only one genuine ghost, and that is in her posthumous novel *Gaston de Blondeville*. As the nineteenth century drew nearer, however, the amount of supernaturalism in the Gothic novel increased, so that by the day of Matthew Gregory Lewis's *The Monk,* super-natural devices included magic, witchcraft, true ghosts who took an active part in the story, a devil, and much else. No apology is made for this weird company.

Walpole's strongest contribution to the Gothic development lies in the inner dynamics of his story. Almost all Gothic novels are motivated in the same way. At some time in the past a crime was committed but was not avenged. The criminal is usually a murderer and usurper. At the time the story takes place the true heir to the usurped estate lies hidden in another identity, unconscious of his destiny. It would seem that he is permanently swindled of his patrimony, and that murder will not out. But the criminal, or villain, persecutes the true heir, and through a chain of circumstances, which usually involve the supernatural, the ancient crime is detected, the villain is punished, and the heir receives his birthright. It might be said that the Gothic novel is a primitive detective story in which God or Fate is the detective.

Gothic novels up through the first decade of the nineteenth century retain this basic plot. But gradually a change occurs in the fleshing of this skeleton. In the earlier novels, as in Walpole's *Castle of Otranto,* the "hero" is a passive character who merely responds to the buffetings of the "villain's" energy until Fate takes a hand. Gradually, in the evolution of the novel, however, the center of interest shifts toward the "villain," who acquires a Mephistotelean, Byronic fascination for the reader. The former "hero" is gradually pushed into the background. By the time of Charles Maturin's *Melmoth the Wanderer* [1820], which is the flower of the Gothic school, the "villain" Melmoth is the center of the story. It might be said that the understanding of evil, within the Gothic novel, has shifted from the Hamlet situation which Walpole recognized he had taken from Shakespeare, to the Lucifer of *Paradise Lost,* on the part of the Protestant clergyman Maturin.

So saturated was the literature of this period with Gothicism that a reaction set in and prose parodies appeared satirizing individual novels or the form in general. Best known of these works (although it contains other elements as well) is Jane Austen's *Northanger Abbey,* where *The Horrid Mysteries, The Necromancer of the Black Forest* and other Gothic novels are mentioned and discussed. William Beckford, the author of *Vathek,* also parodied his half-sister's sentimental Gothic novels with his *Modern Novel Writing* and *Azemia.* Perhaps the best strict parody of the Gothic form, however, is E. S. Barrett's *The Heroine,* which is partly a pastiche of elements from many popular novels. It has been reprinted several times, up to the 1930's, and is still worth reading. Peacock's *Nightmare Abbey*, which is a brilliant burlesque of Romantic ideas of many schools, even brings Coleridge and Byron into a Gothic plot.

A satirical poem by C. J. Pitt, *The Age: A Poem, Moral, Political, and Metaphysical, with Illustrative Annotations* [London, 1810], tells how a Gothic novel may be created; extended footnotes to the poem even give a recipe for transmuting the Gothic apparatus into the sentimental novel:

(1) The conduct of the poet in considering romances and novels separately, may be thought singular by those who have penetration to see that a novel may be made out of a romance, or a romance out of a novel with the greatest ease, by scratching out a few terms, and inserting others. Take the following, which may, like machinery in factories, accelerate the progress of the divine art.

From any romance to make a novel.

Where you find —

A castle,	put An house
A cavern,	A bower
A groan,	A sigh
A giant,	A father
A bloodstained dagger,	A fan
A knight,	A gentleman without whiskers
A lady who is the heroine,	Need not be changed, being versatile.
Assassins,	Telling glances.
A monk,	An old steward.
Skeletons, skulls, &c.	Compliments, sentiments, &c.
A gliding ghost,	A usurer, or an attorney
A midnight murder,	A marriage

The same table of course answers for transmuting a novel into a romance.

Some time later Sir Walter Scott said, in a similar vein, while reviewing a Gothic novel, "We strolled through a variety of castles, each of which was regularly called Il Castello, met with as many captains of Condottieri, heard various ejaculations of Santa Maria and Diabolo; read by a decaying lamp and in a tapestried chamber dozens of legends as stupid as the main history; examined such suites of deserted apartments as might set up a reasonable barrack, and saw as many glimmering lights as would make a respectable illumination." The references are to a novel of Ann Radcliffe's school, but the general conclusions are valid for the earlier Gothic novels.

Terms are relative and classification is sometimes a personal exercise, but it is safe to say that Charles Maturin wrote the last major novels that can be considered Gothic. Later works may still contain medieval castles, supernatural happenings, crimes, persecutions, mistaken identities, anticlericalism and other Gothic motives; but there is so much new material and the authors' intentions and techniques are so changed that referring to these novels as Gothic is pointless and misleading.

If Walpole's chain of immediate succession died with Maturin, Walpole's influence persisted in other areas of literature. Many of the genres and subgenres that arose in the following century are heavily indebted to the tradition that he established. To name only a few of the less obvious forms: The novel of crime and detection, which received its major crystallization before Poe in the work of William Godwin (*Things as They Are, or The Adventures of Caleb Williams* [1794], *Cloudesley* [1830], *Deloraine* [1833]) adds the Gothic concept of crime and persecution to a novel that is primarily a novel of social ideas. The historical novel, too, gradually emerged out of the somewhat nebulous interest in the past that characterized the Gothic tradition. In this case it was Sir Walter Scott who transcended the older form and created a novel of Romantic realism. Even as late as his *Bride of Lammermoor*, however, strong Gothic elements appeared in his work. Many of the nationalistic schools of fiction, such as the Irish, in the work of the Banims, or the American, in the early work of William Gilmore Simms, attempt to strike the Gothic mood with material of local origin. On the Continent, particularly in Germany, the Gothic novel became metamorphosed, on one level, into a novel of symbolism, psychopathology, and ideas, as in the work of E. T. A. Hoffmann. His *Devil's Elixir*, for example, is a fine transformation of Lewis's *Monk*.

In popular literature one sort of thriller of obvious Gothic provenience continued to flourish in England and on the Continent. This was the early Victorian "blood," as composed by George Prest and G. W. M. Reynolds in England, Victor Hugo (as in *Hans of Iceland* and *The Hunchback of Notre Dame*) in

France, and George Lippard (*The Quaker City, or The Monks of Monk Hall*) in America. Theirs was a novel of extremely intricate plot, great range of characters, sentimentalism and cheap emotion, sadism and half-submerged eroticism, hairraising incident (often with supernatural overtones), and as a rule poor craftsmanship. E. S. Turner in his fascinating *Boys Will Be Boys* has traced the gradual degeneration of this form into the juvenile literature of the early twentieth century.

Walpole himself might have been annoyed at the aftermath of his architectural involvement, or he might have felt flattered that generations of readers found his novel interesting. *The Castle of Otranto* is not, of course, a great novel, and it would be absurd to claim greatness for it. But Walpole was an intelligent man and a lively personality, and his individual charm can be perceived in his novel. The question whether his horrors are truly frightening or simply ludicrous is a matter for the individual reader to decide. Still, most authorities would agree that the same sort of thing was probably done better by Ann Radcliffe and M. G. Lewis, and certainly by Charles Maturin.

— E. F. Bleiler

THE CASTLE OF OTRANTO

A Gothic Story

Sir Walter Scott's Introduction

The Castle of Otranto is remarkable not only for the wild interest of the story, but as the first modern attempt to found a tale of amusing fiction upon the basis of the ancient romances of chivalry. The neglect and discredit of these venerable legends had commenced so early as the reign of Queen Elizabeth, when, as we learn from the criticism of the times, Spenser's fairy web was rather approved on account of the mystic and allegorical interpretation, than the plain and obvious meaning of his chivalrous pageant. The drama, which shortly afterwards rose into splendour, and versions from the innumerable novelists of Italy, supplied to the higher class the amusement which their fathers received from the legends of Don Belianis and *The Mirror of Knighthood;* and the huge volumes which were once the pastime of nobles and princes, shorn of their ornaments, and shrunk into abridgements, were banished to the kitchen and nursery, or, at best, to the hall-window of the old-fashioned country manor-house. Under Charles II the prevailing taste for French literature dictated the introduction of those dullest of dull folios, the romances of Calprenède and Scudéry, works which hover between the ancient tale of chivalry and the modern novel. The alliance was so ill conceived, that they retained all the insufferable length and breadth of the prose volumes of chivalry, the same detailed account of reiterated and unvaried combats, the same unnatural and extravagant turn of incident, without the rich and sublime strokes of genius, and vigour of imagination, which often distinguished the early romance; while they exhibited all the sentimental languor and flat love-intrigue of the novel, without being enlivened by its variety of character, just traits of feeling, or acute views of life. Such an ill-imagined species of composition retained its ground longer than might have been expected, only because these romances were called works of entertainment, and there was nothing better to supply their room. Even in the days of the *Spectator,* Clelia, Cleopatra,

and the Grand Cyrus (as that precious folio is christened by its
butcherly translator), were the favourite closet companions of
the fair sex. But this unnatural taste began to give way early in
the eighteenth century; and, about the middle of it, was entirely
superseded by the works of Le Sage, Richardson, Fielding, and
Smollett; so that even the very name of romance, now so venerable in the ear of antiquaries and book-collectors, was almost forgotten at the time *The Castle of Otranto* made its first appearance.

The peculiar situation of Horace Walpole, the ingenious author of this work, was such as gave him a decided predilection for
what may be called the Gothic style, a term which he contributed
not a little to rescue from the bad fame into which it had fallen,
being currently used before his time to express whatever was in
pointed and diametrical opposition to the rules of true taste.

Mr. Walpole, it is needless to remind the reader, was son of that
celebrated minister, who held the reins of government under two
successive monarchs, with a grasp so firm and uncontrolled, that
his power seemed entwined with the rights of the Brunswick family. In such a situation, his sons had necessarily their full share of
that court which is usually paid to the near connections of those
who have the patronage of the state at their disposal. To the feeling of importance inseparable from the object of such attention,
was added the early habit of connecting and associating the interest of Sir Robert Walpole, and even the domestic affairs of his
family, with the parties in the Royal Family of England, and with
the changes in the public affairs of Europe. It is not therefore wonderful, that the turn of Horace Walpole's mind, which was naturally tinged with love of pedigree, and a value for family honours, should have been strengthened in that bias by circumstances
which seemed, as it were, to bind and implicate the fate of his own
house with that of princes, and to give the shields of the Walpoles,
Shorters, and Robsarts from whom he descended, an added dignity unknown to their original owners. If Mr. Walpole ever
founded hopes of raising himself to political eminence, and turning his family importance to advantage in his career, the termina-
tion of his father's power, and the personal change with which he
felt it attended, disgusted him with active life, and early consigned
him to literary retirement. He had, indeed, a seat in parliament
for many years; but, unless upon one occasion, when he vindicated the memory of his father with great dignity and eloquence,

he took no share in the debates of the house, and not much in the
parties which maintained them. The subjects of his study were,
in a great measure, dictated by his habits of thinking and feeling
operating upon an animated imagination, and a mind acute, active, penetrating, and fraught with a great variety of miscellane-
ous knowledge. Travelling had formed his taste for the fine arts;
but his early predilection in favour of birth and rank connected
even these branches of study with that of Gothic history and antiquities. His *Anecdotes of Painting and Engraving* evince many
marks of his favourite pursuits; but his *Catalogue of Royal and
Noble Authors,* and his *Historical Doubts,* we owe entirely to the
antiquary and the genealogist. The former work evinces, in a
particular degree, Mr. Walpole's respect for birth and rank; yet
may, perhaps, be ill calculated to gain much sympathy for either.
It would be difficult, by any process, to select a list of as many ple-
beian authors, containing so very few whose genius was worthy
of commemoration. The *Historical Doubts* are an acute and curious example how minute antiquarian research may shake our
faith in the facts most pointedly averred by general history. It is
remarkable also to observe how, in defending a system which was
probably at first adopted as a mere literary exercise, Mr. Walpole's
doubts acquired, in his eyes, the respectability of certainties, in
which he could not brook controversy.

Mr. Walpole's domestic occupations, as well as his studies, bore
evidence of a taste for English antiquities, which was then uncommon. He loved, as a satirist has expressed it, "to gaze on
Gothic toys through Gothic glass"; and the villa at Strawberry-
Hill, which he chose for his abode, gradually swelled into a feudal
castle, by the addition of turrets, towers, galleries, and corridors,
whose fretted roofs, carved panels, and illuminated windows, were
garnished with the appropriate furniture of scutcheons, armorial-
bearings, shields, tilting lances, and all the panoply of chivalry.
The Gothic order of architecture is now so generally, and, indeed,
indiscriminately used, that we are rather surprised if the country-
house of a tradesman retired from business does not exhibit lance-
olated windows, divided by stone shafts, and garnished by painted
glass, a cupboard in the form of a cathedral-stall, and a pig-house
with a front borrowed from the façade of an ancient chapel. But,
in the middle of the eighteenth century, when Mr. Walpole began to exhibit specimens of the Gothic style, and to show how pat-

terns, collected from cathedrals and monuments, might be applied
to chimney-pieces, ceilings, windows, and balustrades, he did not
comply with the dictates of a prevailing fashion, but pleased his
own taste, and realised his own visions, in the romantic cast of
the mansion which he erected.*

Mr. Walpole's lighter studies were conducted upon the same
principle which influenced his historical researches, and his taste
in architecture. His extensive acquaintance with foreign literature, on which he justly prided himself, was subordinate to his
pursuits as an English antiquary and genealogist, in which he
gleaned subjects for poetry and for romantic fiction, as well as for
historical controversy. These are studies, indeed, proverbially
dull; but it is only when they are pursued by those whose fancies
nothing can enliven. A Horace Walpole, or a Thomas Warton, is
not a mere collector of dry and minute facts, which the general
historian passes over with disdain. He brings with him the torch
of genius, to illuminate the ruins through which he loves to wander; nor does the classic scholar derive more inspiration from the
pages of Virgil, than such an antiquary from the glowing, rich, and
powerful feudal painting of Froissart. His mind being thus stored
with information, accumulated by researches into the antiquities
of the middle ages, and inspired, as he himself informs us, by the
romantic cast of his own habitation, Mr. Walpole resolved to give
the public a specimen of the Gothic style adapted to modern literature, as he had already exhibited its application to modern
architecture.

As, in his model of a Gothic modern mansion, our author had
studiously endeavoured to fit to the purposes of modern conven-
ience, or luxury, the rich, varied, and complicated tracery and
carving of the ancient cathedral, so, in *The Castle of Otranto*, it
was his object to unite the marvellous turn of incident, and im-
posing tone of chivalry, exhibited in the ancient romance, with
that accurate exhibition of human character, and contrast of feelings and passions, which is, or ought to be, delineated in the
modern novel. But Mr. Walpole, being uncertain of the reception
which a work upon so new a plan might experience from the
world, and not caring, perhaps, to encounter the ridicule which

* It is well known that Mr. Walpole composed his beautiful and lively fable
of the Entail upon being asked, whether he did not mean to settle Strawberry-
Hill, when he had completed its architecture and ornaments, upon his family?

would have attended its failure, *The Castle of Otranto* was ushered into the world as a translation from the Italian. It does not seem that the authenticity of the narrative was suspected. Mr. Gray writes to Mr. Walpole, on 30th December, 1764: "I have received *The Castle of Otranto*, and return you my thanks for it. It engages our attention here [*i. e.* at Cambridge], makes some of us cry a little; and all, in general, afraid to go to bed o' nights. We take it for a translation; and should believe it to be a true story, if it were not for St. Nicholas." The friends of the author were probably soon permitted to peep beneath the veil he had thought proper to assume; and, in the second edition, it was altogether withdrawn by a preface, in which the tendency and nature of the work are shortly commented upon and explained. From the following passage, translated from a letter by the author to Madame Deffand, it would seem that he repented of having laid aside his incognito; and, sensitive to criticism, like most dilettante authors, was rather more hurt by the raillery of those who liked not his tale of chivalry, than gratified by the applause of his admirers. "So they have translated my *Castle of Otranto*, probably in ridicule of the author. So be it—however, I beg you will let their raillery pass in silence. Let the critics have their own way; they give me no uneasiness. I have not written the book for the present age, which will endure nothing but *cold common sense.* I confess to you, my dear friend, (and you will think me madder than ever), that this is the only one of my works with which I am myself pleased; I have given reins to my imagination till I became on fire with the visions and feelings which it excited. I have composed it in defiance of rules, of critics, and of philosophers; and it seems to me just so much the better for that very reason. I am even persuaded, that some time hereafter, when taste shall resume the place which philosophy now occupies, my poor *Castle* will find admirers: we have actually a few among us already, for I am just publishing the third edition. I do not say this in order to mendicate your approbation.* I told you from the beginning you would not like the book—your visions are all in a different style. I am not sorry that the translator has given the second preface; the first,

* Madame Deffand had mentioned having read *The Castle of Otranto* twice over; but she did not add a word of approbation. She blamed the translator for giving the second preface, chiefly because she thought it might commit Walpole with Voltaire.

however, accords best with the style of the fiction. I wished it to be believed ancient, and almost everybody was imposed upon." If the public applause, however, was sufficiently qualified by the voice of censure to alarm the feelings of the author, the continued demand for various editions of *The Castle of Otranto* showed how high the work really stood in popular estimation, and probably eventually reconciled Mr. Walpole to the taste of his own age. This Romance has been justly considered not only as the original and model of a peculiar species of composition, but as one of the standard works of our lighter literature. A few remarks both on the book itself, and on the class to which it belongs, have been judged an apposite introduction to an edition of *The Castle of Otranto,* which the publishers have endeavoured to execute in a style of elegance corresponding to the estimation in which they hold the work, and the genius of the author.

It is doing injustice to Mr. Walpole's memory to allege, that all which he aimed at in *The Castle of Otranto* was "the art of exciting surprise and horror"; or, in other words, the appeal to that secret and reserved feeling of love for the marvellous and supernatural, which occupies a hidden corner in almost every one's bosom. Were this all which he had attempted, the means by which he sought to attain his purpose might, with justice, be termed both clumsy and puerile. But Mr. Walpole's purpose was both more difficult of attainment, and more important when attained. It was his object to draw such a picture of domestic life and manners, during the feudal times, as might actually have existed, and to paint it chequered and agitated by the action of supernatural machinery, such as the superstition of the period received as matter of devout credulity. The natural parts of the narrative are so contrived, that they associate themselves with the marvellous occurrences; and, by the force of that association, render those *speciosa miracula* striking and impressive, though our cooler reason admits their impossibility. Indeed to produce, in a well-cultivated mind, any portion of that surprise and fear which is founded on supernatural events, the frame and tenor of the whole story must be adjusted in perfect harmony with this mainspring of the interest. He who, in early youth, has happened to pass a solitary night in one of the few ancient mansions which the fashion of more modern times has left undespoiled of their original furniture, has probably experienced, that the gigantic and preposterous figures dimly visible in the defaced tapestry, the remote clang of the distant doors which divide him from living society, the deep darkness which involves the high and fretted roof of the apartment, the dimly-seen pictures of ancient knights, renowned for their valour, and perhaps for their crimes, the varied and indistinct sounds which disturb the silent desolation of a half-deserted mansion; and, to crown all, the feeling that carries us back to ages of feudal power and papal superstition, join together to excite a corresponding sensation of supernatural awe, if not of terror. It is in such situations, when superstition becomes contagious, that we listen with respect, and even with dread, to the legends which are our sport in the garish light of sun-shine, and amid the dissipating sights and sounds of every-day life. Now it seems to have been Walpole's object to attain, by the minute accuracy of a fable, sketched with singular attention to the costume of the period in which the scene was laid, that same association which might prepare his reader's mind for the reception of prodigies congenial to the creed and feelings of the actors. His feudal tyrant, his distressed damsel, his resigned, yet dignified, churchman—the Castle itself, with its feudal arrangement of dungeons, trap-doors, oratories, and galleries, the incidents of the trial, the chivalrous procession, and the combat—in short, the scene, the performers, and action, so far as it is natural, form the accompaniments of his spectres and his miracles, and have the same effect on the mind of the reader that the appearance and drapery of such a chamber as we have described may produce upon that of a temporary inmate. This was a task which required no little learning, no ordinary degree of fancy, no common portion of genius, to execute. The association of which we have spoken is of a nature peculiarly delicate, and subject to be broken and disarranged. It is, for instance, almost impossible to build such a modern Gothic structure as shall impress us with the feelings we have endeavoured to describe. It may be grand, or it may be gloomy; it may excite magnificent or melancholy ideas; but it must fail in bringing forth the sensation of supernatural awe, connected with halls that have echoed to the sounds of remote generations, and have been pressed by the footsteps of those who have long since passed away. Yet Horace Walpole has attained in composition, what, as an architect, he must have felt beyond the power of his art. The remote and superstitious period in which his scene is laid, the art with which he

has furnished forth its Gothic decorations, the sustained, and, in
general, the dignified tone of feudal manners, prepare us gradually for the favourable reception of prodigies which, though they
could not really have happened at any period, were consistent
with the belief of all mankind at that in which the action is placed.
It was, therefore, the author's object not merely to excite surprise
and terror, by the introduction of supernatural agency, but to
wind up the feelings of his reader till they became for a moment
identified with those of a ruder age, which

Held each strange tale devoutly true.

The difficulty of attaining this nice accuracy of delineation may
be best estimated by comparing *The Castle of Otranto* with the
less successful efforts of later writers; where, amid all their at-
tempts to assume the tone of antique chivalry, something occurs
in every chapter so decidedly incongruous, as at once reminds us
of an ill-sustained masquerade, in which ghosts, knights-errant,
magicians, and damsels gent, are all equipped in hired dresses
from the same warehouse in Tavistock-street.

There is a remarkable particular in which Mr. Walpole's steps
have been departed from by the most distinguished of his followers.

Romantic narrative is of two kinds—that which, being in itself possible, may be matter of belief at any period; and that
which, though held impossible by more enlightened ages, was yet
consonant with the faith of earlier times. The subject of *The
Castle of Otranto* is of the latter class. Mrs. Radcliffe, a name not
to be mentioned without the respect due to genius, has endeavoured to effect a compromise between those different styles of narrative, by referring her prodigies to an explanation, founded on
natural causes, in the latter chapters of her romances. To this im-
provement upon the Gothic romance there are so many objec-
tions, that we own ourselves inclined to prefer, as more simple and
impressive, the narrative of Walpole, which details supernatural
incidents as they would have been readily believed and received
in the eleventh or twelfth century. In the first place, the reader
feels indignant at discovering he has been cheated into a sympathy with terrors which are finally explained as having proceeded
from some very simple cause; and the interest of a second reading
is entirely destroyed by his having been admitted behind the

scenes at the conclusion of the first. Secondly, the precaution of relieving our spirits from the influence of supposed supernatural terror, seems as unnecessary in a work of professed fiction, as that of the prudent Bottom, who proposed that the human face of the representative of his lion should appear from under his masque,* and acquaint the audience plainly that he was a man as other men, and nothing more than Snug the joiner. Lastly, these substitutes for supernatural agency are frequently to the full as improbable as the machinery which they are introduced to explain away and to supplant. The reader, who is required to admit the belief of supernatural interference, understands precisely what is demanded of him; and, if he be a gentle reader, throws his mind into the attitude best adapted to humour the deceit which is presented for his entertainment, and grants, for the time of perusal, the premises on which the fable depends.† But if the author voluntarily binds himself to account for all the wondrous occurrences which he introduces, we are entitled to exact that the explanation shall be natural, easy, ingenious, and complete. Every reader of such works must remember instances in which the explanation of mysterious circumstances in the narrative has proved equally, nay, even more incredible, than if they had been accounted for by the agency of supernatural beings. For the most incredulous must allow, that the interference of such agency is more possible than that an effect resembling it should be produced by an inadequate cause. But it is unnecessary to enlarge further on a part of the subject, which we have only mentioned to exculpate our author from the charge of using machinery more clumsy than his tale

* Honest Bottom's device seems to have been stolen by Mr. John Wiseman, schoolmaster of Linlithgow, who performed a lion in a pageant presented before Charles I, but vindicated his identity in the following verses put into his mouth by Drummond of Hawthornden:

> Thrice royal sir, here do I thee beseech,
> Who art a lion, to hear a lion's speech:
> A miracle! for, since the days of Aesop,
> No lion till those times his voice did raise up
> To such a majesty: Then, King of Men,
> The King of beasts speaks to thee from his den,
> Who, though he now inclosed be in plaster,
> When he was free, was Lithgow's wise schoolmaster.

† There are instances to the contrary however. For example, that stern votary of severe truth, who cast aside *Gulliver's Travels* as containing a parcel of improbable fictions.

from its nature required. The bold assertion of the actual existence of phantoms and apparitions seems to us to harmonise much
more naturally with the manners of feudal times, and to produce
a more powerful effect upon the reader's mind, than any attempt
to reconcile the superstitious credulity of feudal ages with the
philosophic scepticism of our own, by referring those prodigies to
the operation of fulminating powder, combined mirrors, magic
lanthorns, trap-doors, speaking trumpets, and such like apparatus
of German phantasmagoria.

It cannot, however, be denied, that the character of the supernatural machinery in *The Castle of Otranto* is liable to objec-
tions. Its action and interference is rather too frequent, and
presses too hard and constantly upon the same feelings in the
reader's mind, to the hazard of diminishing the elasticity of the
spring upon which it should operate. The fund of fearful sympathy which can be afforded by a modern reader to a tale of
wonder, is much diminished by the present habits of life and
mode of education. Our ancestors could wonder and thrill through
all the mazes of an interminable metrical romance of fairy land,
and of enchantment, the work perhaps of some

> Prevailing poet, whose undoubting mind
> Believed the magic wonders which he sung.

But our habits and feelings and belief are different, and a tran-
sient, though vivid, impression is all that can be excited by a tale
of wonder even in the most fanciful mind of the present day. By
the too frequent recurrence of his prodigies, Mr. Walpole ran,
perhaps, his greatest risk of awakening *la raison froide,* that cold
common sense, which he justly deemed the greatest enemy of the
effect which he hoped to produce. It may be added also, that the
supernatural occurrences of *The Castle of Otranto* are brought
forward into too strong day-light, and marked by an over degree
of distinctness and accuracy of outline. A mysterious obscurity
seems congenial at least, if not essential, to our ideas of disembod-
ied spirits, and the gigantic limbs of the ghost of Alphonso, as
described by the terrified domestics, are somewhat too distinct and
corporeal to produce the feelings which their appearance is intended to excite. This fault, however, if it be one, is more than
compensated by the high merit of many of the marvellous incidents in the romance. The descent of the picture of Manfred's

ancestor, although it borders on extravagance, is finely introduced, and interrupts an interesting dialogue with striking effect. We have heard it observed, that the animated figure should rather have been a statue than a picture. We greatly doubt the justice of the criticism. The advantage of the colouring induces us decidedly to prefer Mr. Walpole's fiction to the proposed substitute. There are few who have not felt, at some period of their childhood, a sort of terror from the manner in which the eye of an ancient portrait appears to fix that of the spectator from every point of view. It is, perhaps, hypercritical to remark (what, however, Walpole of all authors might have been expected to attend to), that the time assigned to the action, being about the eleventh century, is rather too early for the introduction of a full-length portrait. The apparition of the skeleton hermit to the prince of Vicenza was long accounted a master-piece of the horrible; but of late the valley of Jehosophat could hardly supply the dry bones necessary for the exhibition of similar spectres, so that injudicious and repeated imitation has, in some degree, injured the effect of its original model. What is most striking in *The Castle of Otranto,* is the manner in which the various prodigious appearances, bearing each upon the other, and all upon the accomplishment of the ancient prophecy, denouncing the ruin of the house of Manfred, gradually prepare us for the grand catastrophe. The moon-light vision of Alphonso dilated to immense magnitude, the astonished group of spectators in the front, and the shattered ruins of the castle in the back-ground, is briefly and sublimely described. We know no passage of similar merit, unless it be the apparition of Fadzean in an ancient Scottish poem.*

That part of the romance which depends upon human feelings and agency, is conducted with the dramatic talent which afterwards was so conspicuous in *The Mysterious Mother.* The persons are indeed rather generic than individual, but this was in a degree necessary to a plan calculated rather to exhibit a general view of society and manners during the times which the author's imagination loved to contemplate, than the more minute shades and discriminating points of particular characters. But the actors in the romance are strikingly drawn, with bold outlines becoming the

---

* This spectre, the ghost of a follower whom he had slain upon suspicion of treachery, appeared to no less a person than Wallace, the champion of Scotland, in the ancient castle of Gask-hall.—See Ellis's *Specimens,* vol. I.

age and nature of the story. Feudal tyranny was, perhaps, never better exemplified, than in the character of Manfred. He has the courage, the art, the duplicity, the ambition of a barbarous chieftain of the dark ages, yet with touches of remorse and natural feeling, which preserve some sympathy for him when his pride is quelled, and his race extinguished. The pious monk, and the patient Hippolita, are well contrasted with this selfish and tyrannical prince. Theodore is the juvenile hero of a romantic tale, and Matilda has more interesting sweetness than usually belongs to its heroine. As the character of Isabella is studiously kept down, in order to relieve that of the daughter of Manfred, few readers are pleased with the concluding insinuation, that she' became at length the bride of Theodore. This is in some degree a departure from the rules of chivalry; and however natural an occurrence in common life, rather injures the magic illusions of romance. In other respects, making allowance for the extraordinary incidents of a dark and tempestuous age, the story, so far as within the course of natural events, is happily detailed, its progress is uniform, its events interesting and well combined, and the conclusion grand, tragical, and affecting.

The style of *The Castle of Otranto* is pure and correct English of the earlier and more classical standard. Mr. Walpole rejected, upon taste and principle, those heavy though powerful auxiliaries which Dr. Johnson imported from the Latin language, and which have since proved to many a luckless wight, who has essayed to use them, as unmanageable as the gauntlets of Eryx,

———————*et pondus et ipsa*
Huc illuc vinclorum immensa volumina versat.

Neither does the purity of Mr. Walpole's language, and the simplicity of his narrative, admit that luxuriant, florid, and high-varnished landscape painting with which Mrs. Radcliffe often adorned, and not unfrequently encumbered, her kindred romances. Description, for its own sake, is scarcely once attempted in *The Castle of Otranto;* and if authors would consider how very much this restriction tends to realise narrative, they might be tempted to abridge at least the showy and wordy exuberance of a style fitter for poetry than prose. It is for the dialogue that Walpole reserves his strength; and it is remarkable how, while conducting his mortal agents with all the art of a modern dramatist, he adheres to the sustained tone of chivalry, which marks the period of the action. This is not attained by patching his narrative or dialogue with glossarial terms, or antique phraseology, but by taking care to exclude all that can awaken modern associations. In the one case, his romance would have resembled a modern dress, preposterously decorated with antique ornaments; in its present shape, he has retained the form of the ancient armour, but not its rust and cobwebs. In illustration of what is above stated, we refer the reader to the first interview of Manfred with the prince of Vicenza, where the manners and language of chivalry are finely painted, as well as the perturbation of conscious guilt confusing itself in attempted exculpation, even before a mute accuser. The characters of the inferior domestics have been considered as not bearing a proportion sufficiently dignified to the rest of the story. But this is a point on which the author has pleaded his own cause fully in the original prefaces.

We have only to add, in conclusion to these desultory remarks, that if Horace Walpole, who led the way in this new species of literary composition, has been surpassed by some of his followers in diffuse brilliancy of description, and perhaps in the art of detaining the mind of the reader in a state of feverish and anxious suspense, through a protracted and complicated narrative, more will yet remain with him than the single merit of originality and invention. The applause due to chastity and precision of style, to a happy combination of supernatural agency with human interest, to a tone of feudal manners and language, sustained by characters strongly drawn and well discriminated, and to unity of action producing scenes alternately of interest and of grandeur—the applause, in fine, which cannot be denied to him who can excite the passions of fear and of pity, must be awarded to the author of *The Castle of Otranto.*

Preface to the First Edition

The following work was found in the library of an ancient Catholic family in the north of England. It was printed at Naples, in the black letter, in the year 1529. How much sooner it was written does not appear. The principal incidents are such as were believed in the darkest ages of christianity; but the language and conduct have nothing that savours of barbarism. The style is the purest Italian. If the story was written near the time when it is supposed to have happened, it must have been between 1095, the era of the first crusade, and 1243, the date of the last, or not long afterwards. There is no other circumstance in the work, that can lead us to guess at the period in which the scene is laid. The names of the actors are evidently fictitious, and probably disguised on purpose: yet the Spanish names of the domestics seem to indicate that this work was not composed until the establishment of the Arragonian kings in Naples had made Spanish appellations familiar in that country. The beauty of the diction, and the zeal of the author (moderated, however, by singular judgment), concur to make me think, that the date of the composition was little antecedent to that of the impression. Letters were then in their most flourishing state in Italy, and contributed to dispel the empire of superstition, at that time so forcibly attacked by the reformers. It is not unlikely, that an artful priest might endeavour to turn their own arms on the innovators; and might avail himself of his abilities as an author to confirm the populace in their ancient errors and superstitions. If this was his view, he has certainly acted with signal address. Such a work as the following would enslave a hundred vulgar minds, beyond half the books of controversy that have been written from the days of LUTHER to the present hour.

This solution of the author's motives is, however, offered as a mere conjecture. Whatever his views were, or whatever effects the execution of them might have, his work can only be laid before the public at present as a matter of entertainment. Even as such, some apology for it is necessary. Miracles, visions, necromancy, dreams, and other preternatural events, are exploded now even from romances. That was not the case when our author wrote; much less when the story itself is supposed to have happened. Belief in every kind of prodigy was so established in those dark ages, that an author would not be faithful to the manners of the times, who should omit all mention of them. He is not bound to believe them himself, but he must represent his actors as believing them.

If this air of the miraculous is excused, the reader will find nothing else unworthy of his perusal. Allow the possibility of the facts, and all the actors comport themselves as persons would do in their situation. There is no bombast, no similes, flowers, digressions, or unnecessary descriptions. Every thing tends directly to the catastrophe. Never is the reader's attention relaxed. The rules of the drama are almost observed throughout the conduct of the piece. The characters are well drawn, and still better maintained. Terror, the author's principal engine, prevents the story from ever languishing; and it is so often contrasted by pity, that the mind is kept up in a constant vicissitude of interesting passions.

Some persons may, perhaps, think the characters of the domestics too little serious for the general cast of the story; but, besides their opposition to the principal personages, the art of the author is very observable in his conduct of the subalterns. They discover many passages essential to the story, which could not be well brought to light but by their naïveté and simplicity: in particular, the womanish terror and foibles of Bianca, in the last chapter, conduce essentially towards advancing the catastrophe.

It is natural for a translator to be prejudiced in favour of his adopted work. More impartial readers may not be so much struck with the beauties of this piece as I was. Yet I am not blind to my author's defects. I could wish he had grounded his plan on a more useful moral than this: that "the sins of fathers are visited on their children to the third and fourth generation." I doubt whether, in his time, any more than at present, ambition curbed its appetite of dominion from the dread of so remote a punishment. And yet this moral is weakened by that less direct insinuation, that even such anathema may be diverted, by devotion to St. Nicholas. Here, the interest of the monk plainly gets the better of the judgment of the author. However, with all its faults, I have no doubt but the English reader will be pleased with a sight of this performance. The piety that reigns throughout, the lessons of virtue that are inculcated, and the rigid purity of the sentiments, exempt this work from the censure to which romances are but too liable. Should it meet with the success I hope for, I may be encouraged to re-print the original Italian, though it will tend to depreciate my own labour. Our language falls far short of the charms of the Italian, both for variety and harmony. The latter is peculiarly excellent for simple narrative. It is difficult, in English, to relate without falling too low, or rising too high; a fault obviously occasioned by the little care taken to speak pure language in common conversation. Every Italian or Frenchman, of any rank, piques himself on speaking his own tongue correctly and with choice. I cannot flatter myself with having done justice to my author in this respect: his style is as elegant, as his conduct of the passions is masterly. It is a pity that he did not apply his talents to what they were evidently proper for, the theatre.

I will detain the reader no longer, but to make one short remark. Though the machinery is invention, and the names of the actors imaginary, I cannot but believe, that the ground work of the story is founded on truth. The scene is undoubtedly laid in some real castle. The author seems frequently, without design, to describe particular parts. "The chamber," says he, "on the right hand; the door on the left hand; the distance from the chapel to Conrad's apartment." These, and other passages, are strong presumptions that the author had some certain building in his eye. Curious persons, who have leisure to employ in such researches, may possibly discover in the Italian writers the foundation on which our author has built. If a catastrophe, at all resembling that which he describes, is believed to have given rise to this work, it will contribute to interest the reader, and will make *The Castle of Otranto* a still more moving story.

Preface to the Second Edition

The favourable manner in which this little piece has been received by the public, calls upon the author to explain the grounds on which he composed it. But, before he opens those motives, it is fit that he should ask pardon of his readers for having offered his work to them under the borrowed personage of a translator. As diffidence of his own abilities, and the novelty of the attempt, were the sole inducements to assume that disguise, he flatters himself he shall appear excusable. He resigned his performance to the impartial judgment of the public; determined to let it perish in obscurity, if disapproved; nor meaning to avow such a trifle, unless better judges should pronounce that he might own it without a blush.

It was an attempt to blend the two kinds of romance, the ancient and the modern. In the former, all was imagination and improbability: in the latter, nature is always intended to be, and sometimes has been, copied with success. Invention has not been wanting; but the great resources of fancy have been dammed up, by a strict adherence to common life. But if, in the latter species, Nature has cramped imagination, she did but take her revenge, having been totally excluded from old romances. The actions, sentiments, and conversations, of the heroes and heroines of ancient days, were as unnatural as the machines employed to put them in motion.

The author of the following pages thought it possible to reconcile the two kinds. Desirous of leaving the powers of fancy at liberty to expatiate through the boundless realms of invention, and thence of creating more interesting situations, he wished to conduct the mortal agents in his drama according to the rules of probability; in short, to make them think, speak, and act, as it might be supposed mere men and women would do in extraordinary positions. He had observed, that, in all inspired writings, the personages under the dispensation of miracles, and witnesses to the most stupendous phenomena, never lose sight of their human character: whereas, in the productions of romantic story, an improbable event never fails to be attended by an absurd dialogue. The actors seem to lose their senses, the moment the laws of nature have lost their tone. As the public have applauded the attempt, the author must not say he was entirely unequal to the task he had undertaken: yet, if the new route he has struck out shall have paved a road for men of brighter talents, he shall own, with pleasure and modesty, that he was sensible the plan was capable of receiving greater embellishments than his imagination, or conduct of the passions, could bestow on it.

With regard to the deportment of the domestics, on which I have touched in the former preface, I will beg leave to add a few words.—The simplicity of their behaviour, almost tending to excite smiles, which, at first, seems not consonant to the serious cast of the work, appeared to me not only not improper, but was marked designedly in that manner. My rule was nature. However grave, important, or even melancholy, the sensations of princes and heroes may be, they do not stamp the same affections on their domestics: at least the latter do not, or should not be made to, express their passions in the same dignified tone. In my humble opinion, the contrast between the sublime of the one and the naïveté of the other, sets the pathetic of the former in a stronger light. The very impatience which a reader feels, while delayed, by the coarse pleasantries of vulgar actors, from arriving at the knowledge of the important catastrophe he expects, perhaps heightens, certainly proves that he has been artfully interested in, the depending event. But I had higher authority than my own opinion for this conduct. The great master of nature, SHAKE-SPEARE, was the model I copied. Let me ask, if his tragedies of *Hamlet* and *Julius Caesar* would not lose a considerable share of their spirit and wonderful beauties, if the humour of the grave-diggers, the fooleries of Polonius, and the clumsy jests of the Roman citizens, were omitted, or vested in heroics? Is not the eloquence of Antony, the nobler and affectedly-unaffected oration of Brutus, artificially exalted by the rude bursts of nature from the mouths of their auditors? These touches remind one of the Grecian sculptor, who, to convey the idea of a Colossus, within the dimensions of a seal, inserted a little boy measuring his thumb.

"No," says Voltaire, in his edition of Corneille, "this mixture

of buffoonery and solemnity is intolerable."—Voltaire is a genius*
—but not of Shakespeare's magnitude. Without recurring to dis-
putable authority, I appeal from Voltaire to himself. I shall not
avail myself of his former encomiums on our mighty poet; though
the French critic has twice translated the same speech in *Hamlet*,
some years ago in admiration, latterly in derision; and I am sorry
to find that his judgment grows weaker when it ought to be farther matured. But I shall make use of his own words, delivered on
the general topic of the theatre, when he was neither thinking to
recommend or decry Shakespeare's practice; consequently, at a
moment when Voltaire was impartial. In the preface to his *Enfant
Prodigue*, that exquisite piece, of which I declare my admiration,
and which, should I live twenty years longer, I trust I shall never
attempt to ridicule, he has these words, speaking of comedy (but
equally applicable to tragedy, if tragedy is, as surely it ought to
be, a picture of human life; nor can I conceive why occasional
pleasantry ought more to be banished from the tragic scene, than
pathetic seriousness from the comic), "*On y voit un mélange de
sérieux et de plaisanterie, de comique et de touchant; souvent
même une seule aventure produit tous ces contrastes. Rien n'est
si commun qu'une maison dans laquelle* un père gronde, une fille
occupée de sa passion pleure; *le fils se moque des deux, et quel-
ques parents prennent différemment part à la scène, &c. Nous
n'inférons pas de là que toute comédie doive avoir des scènes de
bouffonnerie et des scènes attendrissantes: il y a beaucoup de
très bonnes pièces où il ne règne que de la gaieté; d'autres toutes*

* The following remark is foreign to the present question, yet excusable
in an Englishman, who is willing to think that the severe criticisms of so masterly a writer as Voltaire on our immortal countryman, may have been the effusions of wit and precipitation, rather than the result of judgment and attention. May not the critic's skill, in the force and powers of our language,
have been as incorrect and incompetent as his knowledge of our history? of
the latter, his own pen has dropped glaring evidence. In his Preface to Thomas
Corneille's *Earl of Essex*, Monsieur de Voltaire allows that the truth of history
has been grossly perverted in that piece. In excuse he pleads, that when Corneille wrote, the noblesse of France were much unread in English story; but
now, says the commentator, that they study it, such misrepresentations would
not be suffered—yet forgetting that the period of ignorance is lapsed, and
that it is not very necessary to instruct the knowing, he undertakes, from the
overflowing of his own reading, to give the nobility of his own country a detail of Queen Elizabeth's favourites—of whom, says he, Robert Dudley was the
first, and the Earl of Leicester the second. Could one have believed that it
could be necessary to inform Monsieur de Voltaire himself, that Robert Dudley and the Earl of Leicester were the same person?

*sérieuses; d'autres mélangées: d'autres où l'attendrissement va
jusques aux larmes:* il ne faut donner l'exclusion à aucun genre;
*et si on me demandoit, quel genre est le meilleur, je répondrois,
celui qui est le mieux traité."* Surely if a comedy may be *toute sé-
rieuse,* tragedy may now and then, soberly, be indulged in a smile.
Who shall proscribe it? Shall the critic, who, in self-defence, declares, that *no kind* ought to be excluded from comedy, give laws
to Shakespeare?

I am aware that the preface from whence I have quoted these
passages does not stand in Monsieur de Voltaire's name, but in
that of his editor; yet who doubts that the editor and author were
the same person? or where is the editor, who has so happily possessed himself of his author's style, and brilliant ease of argument?
These passages were indubitably the genuine sentiments of that
great writer. In his epistle to Maffei, prefixed to his *Mérope,* he
delivers almost the same opinion, though, I doubt, with a little
irony. I will repeat his words, and then give my reason for quot-
ing them. After translating a passage in Maffei's *Merope,* Monsieur de Voltaire adds, *"Tous ces traits sont naïfs; tout y est con-
venable à ceux que vous introduisez sur la scène,* et aux moeurs
que vous leur donnez. *Ces familiarités naturelles eussent été,
à ce que je crois, bien reçues dans Athènes; mais Paris et notre
parterre veulent une autre espèce de simplicité."* I doubt, I say,
whether there is not a grain of sneer in this and other passages of that epistle; yet the force of truth is not damaged by being tinged with ridicule. Maffei was to represent a Grecian story:
surely the Athenians were as competent judges of Grecian manners, and of the propriety of introducing them, as the parterre of
Paris. "On the contrary," says Voltaire (and I cannot but admire
his reasoning), "there were but ten thousand citizens at Athens,
and Paris has near eight hundred thousand inhabitants, among
whom one may reckon thirty thousand judges of dramatic works."
—Indeed!—but allowing so numerous a tribunal, I believe this
is the only instance in which it was ever pretended that thirty
thousand persons, living near two thousand years after the era in
question, were, upon the mere face of the poll, declared better
judges than the Grecians themselves, of what ought to be the manners of a tragedy written on a Grecian story.

I will not enter into a discussion of the *espèce de simplicité,*
which the parterre of Paris demands, nor of the shackles with

which *the thirty thousand judges* have cramped their poetry, the chief merit of which, as I gather from repeated passages in the *New Commentary* on Corneille, consists in vaulting in spite of those fetters; a merit which, if true, would reduce poetry from the lofty effort of imagination, to a puerile and most contemptible labour—*difficiles nugae* with a witness! I cannot, however, help mentioning a couplet, which, to my English ears, always sounded as the flattest and most trifling instance of circumstantial propriety, but which Voltaire, who has dealt so severely with nine parts in ten of Corneille's works, has singled out to defend in Racine;

> *De son appartement cette porte est prochaine,*
> *Et cette autre conduit dans celui de la Reine.*

IN ENGLISH.
To Caesar's closet through this door you come,
And t'other leads to the Queen's drawing-room.

Unhappy Shakespeare! hadst thou made Rosencrantz inform his compeer, Guildenstern, of the ichnography of the palace of Copenhagen, instead of presenting us with a moral dialogue between the Prince of Denmark and the grave-digger, the illuminated pit of Paris would have been instructed *a second time* to adore thy talents.

The result of all I have said, is, to shelter my own daring under the canon of the brightest genius this country, at least, has produced. I might have pleaded that, having created a new species of romance, I was at liberty to lay down what rules I thought fit for the conduct of it: but I should be more proud of having imitated, however faintly, weakly, and at a distance, so masterly a pattern, than to enjoy the entire merit of invention, unless I could have marked my work with genius, as well as with originality. Such as it is, the public have honoured it sufficiently, whatever rank their suffrages allot to it.

THE CASTLE OF OTRANTO

A Gothic Story

CHAPTER I

Manfred, Prince of Otranto, had one son and one daughter; the latter, a most beautiful virgin, aged eighteen, was called Matilda. Conrad, the son, was three years younger, a homely youth, sickly, and of no promising disposition; yet he was the darling of his father, who never showed any symptoms of affection to Matilda. Manfred had contracted a marriage for his son with the Marquis of Vicenza's daughter, Isabella; and she had already been delivered by her guardians into the hands of Manfred, that he might celebrate the wedding as soon as Conrad's infirm state of health would permit. Manfred's impatience for this ceremonial was remarked by his family and neighbours. The former, indeed, apprehending the severity of their prince's disposition, did not dare to utter their surmises on this precipitation. Hippolita, his wife, an amiable lady, did sometimes venture to represent the danger of marrying their only son so early, considering his great youth, and greater infirmities; but she never received any other answer than reflections on her own sterility, who had given him but one heir. His tenants and subjects were less cautious in their discourses: they attributed this hasty wedding to the prince's dread of seeing accomplished an ancient prophecy, which was said to have pronounced, that *the Castle and Lordship of Otranto should pass from the present family whenever the real owner should be grown too large to inhabit it.* It was difficult to make any sense of this prophecy; and still less easy to conceive what it had to do with the marriage in question. Yet these mysteries, or contradictions, did not make the populace adhere the less to their opinion.

Young Conrad's birth-day was fixed for his espousals. The company was assembled in the chapel of the castle, and everything ready for beginning the divine office, when Conrad himself was missing. Manfred, impatient of the least delay, and who had not observed his son retire, dispatched one of his attendants to summon the young prince. The servant, who had not stayed long enough to have crossed the court to Conrad's apartment, came running back breathless, in a frantic manner, his eyes staring, and foaming at the mouth. He said nothing, but pointed to the court. The company were struck with terror and amazement. The princess Hippolita, without knowing what was the matter, but anxious for her son, swooned away. Manfred, less apprehensive than enraged at the procrastination of the nuptials, and at the folly of his domestic, asked imperiously, what was the matter? The fellow made no answer, but continued pointing towards the court-yard; and, at last, after repeated questions put to him, cried out, "Oh! the helmet! the helmet!" In the mean time, some of the company had run into the court, from whence was heard a confused noise of shrieks, horror, and surprise. Manfred, who began to be alarmed at not seeing his son, went himself, to get information of what occasioned this strange confusion. Matilda remained, endeavouring to assist her mother; and Isabella stayed for the same purpose, and to avoid showing any impatience for the bridegroom, for whom, in truth, she had conceived little affection.

The first thing, that struck Manfred's eyes, was a group of his servants, endeavouring to raise something, that appeared to him a mountain of sable plumes. He gazed, without believing his sight. "What are ye doing?" cried Manfred, wrathfully; "where is my son?" A volley of voices replied, "Oh! my lord! the prince! the prince! the helmet! the helmet!" Shocked with these lamentable sounds, and dreading he knew not what, he advanced hastily; but, what a sight for a father's eyes! he beheld his child dashed to pieces, and almost buried under an enormous helmet, a hundred times more large than any casque ever made for human being, and shaded with a proportionable quantity of black feathers.

The horror of the spectacle, the ignorance of all around how this misfortune had happened, and, above all, the tremendous phenomenon before him, took away the prince's speech. Yet his silence lasted longer than even grief could occasion. He fixed his eyes on what he wished in vain to believe a vision; and seemed less attentive to his loss, than buried in meditation on the stupendous object that had occasioned it. He touched, he examined, the fatal casque; nor could even the bleeding mangled remains of the young prince, divert the eyes of Manfred from the portent before him. All, who had known his partial fondness for young Conrad, were as much surprised at their prince's insensibility, as thunderstruck themselves at the miracle of the helmet. They conveyed the disfigured corpse into the hall, without receiving the least direction from Manfred. As little was he attentive to the ladies who remained in the chapel: on the contrary, without mentioning the unhappy princesses, his wife and daughter, the first sounds that dropped from Manfred's lips were, "take care of the Lady Isabella."

The domestics, without observing the singularity of this direction, were guided by their affection to their mistress, to consider it as peculiarly addressed to her situation, and flew to her assistance. They conveyed her to her chamber, more dead than alive, and indifferent to all the strange circumstances she heard, except the death of her son. Matilda, who doted on her mother, smothered her own grief and amazement, and thought of nothing but assisting and comforting her afflicted parent. Isabella, who had been treated by Hippolita like a daughter, and who returned that tenderness with equal duty and affection, was scarce less assiduous about the princess; at the same time, endeavouring to partake and lessen the weight of sorrow which she saw Matilda strove to suppress, for whom she had conceived the warmest sympathy of friendship. Yet her own situation could not help finding its place in her thoughts. She felt no concern for the death of young Conrad, except commiseration; and she was not sorry to be delivered from a marriage, which had promised her little felicity, either from her destined bridegroom, or from the severe temper of Manfred; who, though he had distinguished her by great indulgence, had impressed her mind with terror, from his causeless rigour to such amiable princesses as Hippolita and Matilda.

While the ladies were conveying the wretched mother to her bed, Manfred remained in the court, gazing on the ominous casque, and regardless of the crowd, which the strangeness of the event had now assembled around him. The few words he articulated, tended solely to inquiries, whether any man knew from whence it could have come? Nobody could give him the least information. However, as it seemed to be the sole object of his curiosity, it soon became so to the rest of the spectators, whose conjectures were as absurd and improbable, as the catastrophe itself was unprecedented. In the midst of their senseless guesses, a young peasant, whom rumour had drawn thither from a neighbouring village, observed, that the miraculous helmet was exactly like that on the figure in black marble of Alfonso the Good, one of their former princes, in the church of St. Nicholas. "Villain! what sayest thou?" cried Manfred, starting from his trance in a tempest of rage, and seizing the young man by the collar; "how darest thou utter such treason? thy life shall pay for it." The spectators, who as little comprehended the cause of the prince's fury as all the rest they had seen, were at a loss to unravel this new circumstance. The young peasant himself was still more astonished, not conceiving how he had offended the prince: yet, recollecting himself, with a mixture of grace and humility, he disengaged himself from Manfred's grip, and then, with an obeisance, which discovered more jealousy of innocence, than dismay, he asked, with respect, of what he was guilty? Manfred, more enraged at the vigour, however decently exerted, with which the young man had shaken off his hold, than appeased by his submission, ordered his attendants to seize him; and, if he had not been withheld by his friends, whom he had invited to the nuptials, would have poignarded the peasant in their arms.

During this altercation, some of the vulgar spectators had run to the great church, which stood near the castle, and came back open-mouthed, declaring, that the helmet was missing from Alfonso's statue. Manfred, at this news, grew perfectly frantic; and, as if he sought a subject on which to vent the tempest within him, he rushed again on the young peasant, crying, "Villain! monster! sorcerer! 'tis thou hast done this! 'tis thou hast slain my son!" The mob, who wanted some object within the scope of their capacities, on whom they might discharge their bewildered reasonings, caught the words from the mouth of their lord, and re-echoed, "Aye, aye; 'tis he! 'tis he! He has stolen the helmet from good Alfonso's tomb, and dashed out the brains of our young prince with it!" never reflecting, how enormous the disproportion was between the marble helmet that had been in the church, and that of steel before their eyes; nor, how impossible it was for a youth, seemingly not twenty, to wield a piece of armour of so prodigious a weight.

The folly of these ejaculations brought Manfred to himself: yet, whether provoked at the peasant having observed the resemblance between the two helmets, and thereby led to the farther discovery of the absence of that in the church; or wishing to bury any fresh rumour under so impertinent a supposition; he gravely pronounced that the young man was certainly a necromancer, and that, till the church could take cognizance of the affair, he would have the magician, whom they had thus detected, kept prisoner under the helmet itself, which he ordered his attendants to raise, and place the young man under it; declaring, he should be kept there without food, with which his own infernal art might furnish him.

It was in vain for the youth to represent against this preposterous sentence: in vain did Manfred's friends endeavour to divert him from this savage and ill-grounded resolution. The generality were charmed with their lord's decision, which, to their apprehensions, carried great appearance of justice; as the magician was to be punished by the very instrument with which he had offended: nor were they struck with the least compunction at the probability of the youth being starved; for they firmly believed, that, by his diabolical skill, he could easily supply himself with nutriment.

Manfred thus saw his commands even cheerfully obeyed; and, appointing a guard, with strict orders to prevent any food being conveyed to the prisoner, he dismissed his friends and attendants, and retired to his own chamber, after locking the gates of the castle, in which he suffered none but his domestics to remain.

In the mean time, the care and zeal of the young ladies had brought the princess Hippolita to herself, who, amidst the transports of her own sorrow, frequently demanded news of her lord; would have dismissed her attendants to watch over him, and at last enjoined Matilda to leave her, and visit and comfort her father. Matilda, who wanted no affectionate duty to Manfred, though she trembled at his austerity, obeyed the orders of Hippolita, whom she tenderly recommended to Isabella; and, enquiring of the domestics for her father, was informed, that he was retired to his chamber, and had commanded that nobody should have admittance to him. Concluding that he was immersed in

sorrow for the death of her brother, and fearing to renew his
tears by the sight of his sole remaining child, she hesitated whether
she should break in upon his affliction; yet, solicitude for him,
backed by the commands of her mother, encouraged her to
venture disobeying the orders he had given; a fault she had never
been guilty of before. The gentle timidity of her nature made
her pause for some minutes at his door. She heard him traverse
his chamber, backwards and forwards, with disordered steps; a
mood which increased her apprehensions. She was, however, just
going to beg admittance, when Manfred suddenly opened the
door; and, as it was now twilight, concurring with the disorder of
his mind, he did not distinguish the person, but asked angrily,
who it was? Matilda replied, trembling, "My dearest father, it is
I, your daughter." Manfred, stepping back hastily, cried, "Begone!
I do not want a daughter"; and, flinging back abruptly, clapped
the door against the terrified Matilda.

She was too well acquainted with her father's impetuosity, to
venture a second intrusion. When she had a little recovered the
shock of so bitter a reception, she wiped away her tears, to prevent the additional stab that the knowledge of it would give to
Hippolita, who questioned her, in the most anxious terms, on the
health of Manfred, and how he bore his loss. Matilda assured her
he was well, and supported his misfortune with manly fortitude.
"But, will he not let me see him?" said Hippolita, mournfully;
"will he not permit me to blend my tears with his, and shed a
mother's sorrows in the bosom of her lord? or do you deceive me,
Matilda? I know how Manfred doted on his son: is not the stroke
too heavy for him? has he not sunk under it? You do not answer
me; alas! I dread the worst! Raise me, my maidens; I will, I will,
see my lord. Bear me to him instantly: he is dearer to me even
than my children!" Matilda made signs to Isabella to prevent
Hippolita's rising; and both those lovely young women were using
their gentle violence to stop and calm the princess, when a servant, on the part of Manfred, arrived, and told Isabella, that his
lord demanded to speak with her.

"With me!" cried Isabella. "Go," said Hippolita, relieved by a
message from her lord. "Manfred cannot support the sight of his
own family. He thinks you less disordered than we are, and dreads
the shock of my grief. Console him, dear Isabella; and tell him, I
will smother my own anguish rather than add to his."

As it was now evening, the servant, who conducted Isabella, bore a torch before her. When they came to Manfred, who was walking impatiently about the gallery, he started, and said hastily, "Take away that light, and begone!" Then, shutting the door impetuously, he flung himself upon a bench against the wall, and bade Isabella sit by him. She obeyed, trembling. "I sent for you, lady—" said he, and then stopped, under great appearance of confusion. "My lord!" "Yes, I sent for you on a matter of great moment," resumed he; "dry your tears, young lady. You have lost your bridegroom—yes, cruel fate! and I have lost the hopes of my race! but Conrad was not worthy of your beauty." "How! my lord!" said Isabella; "sure you do not suspect me of not feeling the concern I ought! my duty and affection would have always"—"Think no more of him," interrupted Manfred; "he was a sickly, puny child; and heaven has perhaps taken him away, that I might not trust the honours of my house on so frail a foundation. The line of Manfred calls for numerous supports. My foolish fondness for that boy blinded the eyes of my prudence; but it is better as it is. I hope, in a few years, to have reason to rejoice at the death of Conrad."

Words cannot paint the astonishment of Isabella. At first, she apprehended that grief had disordered Manfred's understanding. Her next thought suggested, that this strange discourse was designed to ensnare her: she feared that Manfred had perceived her indifference for his son; and, in consequence of that idea, she replied, "Good my lord, do not doubt my tenderness! my heart would have accompanied my hand. Conrad would have engrossed all my care; and wherever fate shall dispose of me, I shall always cherish his memory, and regard your highness, and the virtuous Hippolita, as my parents." "Curse on Hippolita!" cried Manfred. "Forget her from this moment, as I do. In short, lady, you have missed a husband undeserving of your charms: they shall now be better disposed of. Instead of a sickly boy, you shall have a husband in the prime of his age, who will know how to value your beauties, and who may expect a numerous offspring." "Alas! my lord," said Isabella, "my mind is too sadly engrossed, by the recent catastrophe in your family, to think of another marriage. If ever my father returns, and it shall be his pleasure, I shall obey, as I did when I consented to give my hand to your son: but until his return, permit me to remain under your hospitable roof, and employ the melancholy hours in assuaging yours, Hippolita's, and the fair Matilda's affliction."

"I desired you once before," said Manfred, angrily, "not to name that woman: from this hour she must be a stranger to you, as she must be to me; in short, Isabella, since I cannot give you my son, I offer you myself." "Heavens!" cried Isabella, waking from her delusion, "what do I hear! you, my lord! you! my father-in-law! the father of Conrad! the husband of the virtuous and tender Hippolita!"—"I tell you," said Manfred, imperiously, "Hippolita is no longer my wife; I divorce her from this hour. Too long has she cursed me by her unfruitfulness. My fate depends on having sons; and this night, I trust, will give a new date to my hopes." At these words he seized the cold hand of Isabella, who was half dead with fright and horror. She shrieked, and started from him. Manfred rose to pursue her; when the moon, which was now up, and gleamed in at the opposite casement, presented to his sight the plumes of the fatal helmet, which rose to the height of the windows, waving backwards and forwards in a tempestuous manner, and accompanied with a hollow and rustling sound. Isabella, who gathered courage from her situation, and who dreaded nothing so much as Manfred's pursuit of his declaration, cried, "Look! my lord! see! Heaven itself declares against your impious intentions!"—"Heaven nor hell shall impede my designs!" said Manfred, advancing again to seize the princess. At that instant, the portrait of his grandfather, which hung over the bench where they had been sitting, uttered a deep sigh, and heaved its breast. Isabella, whose back was turned to the picture, saw not the motion, nor whence the sound came; but started, and said, "Hark, my lord! what sound was that?" and, at the same time, made towards the door. Manfred, distracted between the flight of Isabella, who had now reached the stairs, and yet unable to keep his eyes from the picture, which began to move, had, however, advanced some steps after her, still looking backwards on the portrait, when he saw it quit its panel, and descend on the floor, with a grave and melancholy air. "Do I dream?" cried Manfred, returning; "or are the devils themselves in league against me? Speak, infernal spectre! or, if thou art my grandsire, why dost thou too conspire against thy wretched descendant, who too dearly pays for"—ere he could finish the sentence, the vision sighed again, and made a sign to Manfred to follow him. "Lead on!" cried Manfred; "I will follow thee to the gulf of perdition!" The spectre marched sedately, but dejected, to the end of the gallery, and turned into a chamber on the right hand. Manfred accompanied him at a little distance, full of anxiety and horror, but resolved. As he would have entered the chamber, the door was clapped to with violence by an invisible hand. The prince, collecting courage from this delay, would have forcibly burst open the door with his foot, but found that it resisted his utmost efforts. "Since hell will not satisfy my curiosity," said Manfred, "I will use the human means in my power for preserving my race; Isabella shall not escape me."

That lady, whose resolution had given way to terror the moment she had quitted Manfred, continued her flight to the bottom of the principal stair-case. There she stopped, not knowing whither to direct her steps, nor how to escape from the impetuosity of the prince. The gates of the castle, she knew, were locked, and guards placed in the court. Should she, as her heart prompted her, go and prepare Hippolita for the cruel destiny that awaited her? she did not doubt but Manfred would seek her there, and that his violence would incite him to double the injury he meditated, without leaving room for them to avoid the impetuosity of his passions. Delay might give him time to reflect on the horrid measures he had conceived, or produce some circumstance in her favour, if she could, for that night at least, avoid his odious purpose. Yet, where conceal herself! how avoid the pursuit he would infallibly make throughout the castle! As these thoughts passed rapidly through her mind, she recollected a subterraneous passage, which led from the vaults of the castle to the church of St. Nicholas. Could she reach the altar before she was overtaken, she knew even Manfred's violence would not dare to profane the sacredness of the place; and she determined, if no other means of deliverance offered, to shut herself up for ever among the holy virgins, whose convent was contiguous to the cathedral. In this resolution, she seized a lamp, that burned at the foot of the stair-case, and hurried towards the secret passage.

The lower part of the castle was hollowed into several intricate cloisters; and it was not easy for one, under so much anxiety, to find the door that opened into the cavern. An awful silence reigned throughout those subterraneous regions, except, now and then, some blasts of wind that shook the doors she had passed, and which, grating on the rusty hinges, were re-echoed through that long labyrinth of darkness. Every murmur struck her with new terror; yet more she dreaded to hear the wrathful voice of Manfred, urging his domestics to pursue her. She trod as softly as impatience would give her leave, yet frequently stopped, and listened to hear if she was followed. In one of those moments she thought she heard a sigh. She shuddered, and recoiled a few paces. In a moment she thought she heard the step of some person. Her blood curdled; she concluded it was Manfred. Every suggestion, that horror could inspire, rushed into her mind. She condemned her rash flight, which had thus exposed her to his rage, in a place where her cries were not likely to draw anybody to her assistance. Yet the sound seemed not to come from behind; if Manfred knew where she was, he must have followed her: she was still in one of the cloisters, and the steps she had heard were too distinct to proceed from the way she had come. Cheered with this reflection, and hoping to find a friend in whoever was not the prince, she was going to advance, when a door, that stood a-jar, at some distance to the left, was opened gently; but, e'er her lamp, which she held up, could discover who opened it, the person retreated precipitately, on seeing the light.

Isabella, whom every incident was sufficient to dismay, hesitated whether she should proceed. Her dread of Manfred soon outweighed every other terror. The very circumstance of the person avoiding her, gave her a sort of courage. It could only be, she thought, some domestic belonging to the castle. Her gentleness had never raised her an enemy, and conscious innocence made her hope, that, unless sent by the prince's order to seek her, his servants would rather assist than prevent her flight. Fortifying herself with these reflections, and believing, by what she could observe, that she was near the mouth of the subterraneous cavern, she approached the door that had been opened; but a sudden gust of wind, that met her at the door, extinguished her lamp, and left her in total darkness.

Words cannot paint the horror of the princess's situation. Alone, in so dismal a place, her mind impressed with all the terrible events of the day, hopeless of escaping, expecting every moment the arrival of Manfred, and far from tranquil on knowing she was within reach of somebody, she knew not whom, who for some cause seemed concealed thereabouts; all these thoughts crowded on her distracted mind, and she was ready to sink under her apprehensions. She addressed herself to every saint in heaven, and inwardly implored their assistance. For a considerable time she remained in an agony of despair. At last, as softly as was possible, she felt for the door; and, having found it, entered trembling into the vault, from whence she had heard the sigh and steps. It gave her a kind of momentary joy to perceive an imperfect ray of clouded moonshine gleam from the roof of the vault, which seemed to be fallen in, and from whence hung a fragment of earth or building, she could not distinguish which, that appeared to have been crushed inwards. She advanced eagerly towards this chasm, when she discerned a human form, standing close against the wall.

She shrieked, believing it the ghost of her betrothed Conrad. The figure, advancing, said in a submissive voice, "Be not alarmed, lady: I will not injure you." Isabella, a little encouraged by the words, and tone of voice, of the stranger, and recollecting that this must be the person who had opened the door, recovered her spirits enough to reply, "Sir, whoever you are, take pity on a wretched princess, standing on the brink of destruction! Assist me to escape from this fatal castle, or in a few moments I may be made miserable for ever!" "Alas!" said the stranger, "what can I do to assist you? I will die in your defence; but I am unacquainted with the castle, and want——" "Oh!" said Isabella, hastily interrupting him, "help me but to find a trap-door, that must be hereabout, and it is the greatest service you can do me, for I have not a minute to lose." Saying these words, she felt about on the pavement, and directed the stranger to search likewise, for a smooth piece of brass, inclosed in one of the stones. "That," said she, "is the lock, which opens with a spring, of which I know the secret. If we can find that, I may escape; if not, alas! courteous stranger, I fear I shall have involved you in my misfortunes: Manfred will suspect you for the accomplice of my flight, and you will fall a victim to his resentment." "I value not my life," said the stranger, "and it will be some comfort to lose it in trying to deliver you from his tyranny." "Generous youth!" said Isabella, "how shall I ever requite"—as she uttered these words, a ray of moonshine, streaming through a cranny of the ruin above, shone directly on the lock they sought. "Oh! transport!" said Isabella, "here is the trap-door!" and, taking out a key, she touched the spring, which, starting aside, discovered an iron ring. "Lift up the door," said the princess. The stranger obeyed; and beneath appeared some stone steps, descending into a vault totally dark. "We must go down here," said Isabella: "follow me; dark and dismal as it is, we cannot miss our way; it leads directly to the church of St. Nicholas. But perhaps," added the princess, modestly, "you have no reason to leave the castle, nor have I further occasion for your service; in a few minutes I shall be safe from Manfred's rage—only let me know, to whom I am so much obliged?" "I will never quit you," said the stranger, eagerly, "until I have placed you in safety—nor think me, princess, more generous than I am; though you are my principal care"—the stranger was interrupted by a sudden noise of voices, that seemed approaching, and they soon distinguished these words: "Talk not to me of necromancers! I tell you she must be in the castle; I will find her in spite of enchantment." "Oh! heavens!" cried Isabella, "it is the voice of Manfred! make haste, or we are ruined! and shut the trap-door after you." Saying this, she descended the steps precipitately, and, as the stranger hastened to follow her, he let the door slip out of his hands; it fell, and the spring closed over it. He tried in vain to open it, not having observed Isabella's method of touching the spring; nor had he many moments to make an essay.—The noise of the falling door had been heard by Manfred, who, directed by the sound, hastened thither, attended by his servants with torches. "It must be Isabella," cried Manfred, before he entered the vault; "she is escaping by the subterraneous passage, but she cannot have got far." What was the astonishment of the prince, when, instead of Isabella, the light of the torches discovered to him the young peasant, whom he thought confined under the fatal helmet! "Traitor!" said Manfred, "how camest thou here? I thought thee in durance above in the court." "I am no traitor," replied the young man, boldly, "nor am I answerable for your thoughts."—"Presumptuous villain!" cried Manfred, "dost thou provoke my wrath? tell me; how hast thou escaped from above? thou hast corrupted thy guards, and their lives shall answer it."—"My poverty," said the peasant calmly, "will disculpate them: though the ministers of a tyrant's wrath, to thee they are faithful, and but too willing to execute the orders which you unjustly imposed upon them." "Art thou so hardy as to dare my vengeance?" said the prince; "but tortures shall force the truth from thee. Tell me! I will know thy accomplices." "There was my accomplice!" said the youth, smiling, and pointing to the roof. Manfred ordered the torches to be held up, and perceived that one of the cheeks of the enchanted casque had forced its way through the pavement of the court, as his servants had let it fall over the peasant, and had broken through into the vault, leaving a gap, through which the peasant had pressed himself some minutes before he was found by Isabella. "Was that the way by which thou didst descend?" said Manfred. "It was," said the youth.— "But what noise was that," said Manfred, "which I heard as I entered the cloister?"—"A door clapped," said the peasant; "I heard it as well as you." "What door?" said Manfred, hastily. "I am not acquainted with your castle," said the peasant; "this is the first time I ever entered it; and this vault the only part of it within which I ever was." "But I tell thee," said Manfred (wishing to find out if the youth had discovered the trap-door), "it was this way I heard the noise: my servants heard it too." "My lord," interrupted one of them, officiously, "to be sure it was the trap-door, and he was going to make his escape." "Peace! blockhead!" said the prince, angrily; "if he was going to escape, how should he come on this side? I will know from his own mouth what noise it was I heard. Tell me truly! thy life depends on thy veracity." "My veracity is dearer to me than my life," said the peasant, "nor would I purchase the one by forfeiting the other." "Indeed! young philosopher!" said Manfred, contemptuously; "tell me, then, what was the noise I heard?" "Ask me what I can answer," said he, "and put me to death instantly if I tell you a lie." Manfred, growing impatient at the steady valour and indifference of the youth, cried, "Well then, thou man of truth! answer; was it the fall of the trap-door that I heard?" "It was," said the youth. "It was!" said the prince, "and how didst thou come to know there was a trap-door here?" "I saw the plate of brass by a gleam of moonshine," replied he. "But what told thee it was a lock?" said Manfred; "how didst thou discover the secret of opening it?" "Providence, that delivered me from the helmet, was able to direct me to the spring of a lock," said he. "Providence should have gone a little farther, and have placed thee out of the reach of my resentment," said Manfred; "when Providence had taught thee to open the lock, it abandoned thee for a fool, who did not know how to make use of its favours. Why didst thou not pursue the path pointed out for thy escape? why didst thou shut the trap-door, before thou hadst descended the steps?" "I might ask you, my lord," said the peasant, "how I, totally unacquainted with your castle, was to know that those steps led to any outlet? but I scorn to evade your questions. Wherever those steps led to, perhaps I should have explored the way—I could not be in a worse situation than I was. But the truth is, I let the trap-door fall: your immediate arrival followed. I had given the alarm—what imported it to me whether I was seized a minute sooner or a minute later?" "Thou art a resolute villain, for thy years," said Manfred; "yet, on reflection, I suspect thou dost but trifle with me: thou has not yet told me how thou didst open the lock?" "That I will show you, my lord," said the peasant; and, taking up a fragment of stone that had fallen from above, he laid himself on the trap-door, and began to beat on the piece of brass that covered it; meaning to gain time for the escape of the princess. This presence of mind, joined to the frankness of the youth, staggered Manfred. He even felt a disposition towards pardoning one, who had been guilty of no crime. Manfred was not one of those savage tyrants, who wanton in cruelty unprovoked. The circumstances of his fortune had given an asperity to his temper, which was naturally humane; and his virtues were always ready to operate, when his passions did not obscure his reason.

While the prince was in this suspense, a confused noise of voices echoed through the distant vaults. As the sound approached, he distinguished the clamours of some of his domestics, whom he had dispersed through the castle in search of Isabella, calling out, "Where is my lord? where is the prince?" "Here I am," said Manfred, as they came nearer; "have you found the princess?" the first that arrived, replied, "Oh! my lord! I am glad we have found you!" "Found me!" said Manfred, "have you found the princess?" "We thought we had, my lord," said the fellow, looking terrified, "but"—"But what?" cried the prince; "has she escaped?" "Jaquez, and I, my lord"—"Yes, I and Diego," interrupted the second, who came up in still greater consternation—"Speak one of you at a time!" said Manfred; "I ask you where is the princess?" "We do not know," said they, both together, "but we are frightened out of our wits!"—"So I think, blockheads," said Manfred; "what is it has scared you thus?" "Oh! my lord," said Jaquez, "Diego has seen such a sight! your highness would not believe your eyes"—"What new absurdity is this?" cried Manfred; "give me a direct answer, or by heaven"—"Why, my lord, if it please your highness to hear me," said the poor fellow, "Diego and I"—"Yes, I and Jaquez," cried his comrade—"Did not I forbid you to speak both at a time?" said the prince; "You, Jaquez, answer; for the other fool seems more distracted than thou art. What is the matter?" "My gracious lord," said Jaquez, "if it please your highness to hear me. Diego and I, according to your highness's orders, went to search for the young lady; but, being apprehensive that we might meet the ghost of my young lord, your highness's son, God rest his soul, as he has not received christian burial"—"Sot!" cried Manfred, in a rage, "is it only a ghost, then, that thou hast seen?" "Oh! worse! worse! my lord," cried Diego; "I had rather have seen ten whole ghosts." "Grant me patience!" said Manfred, "these blockheads distract me. Out of my sight, Diego! and thou, Jaquez, tell me, in one word, art thou sober? art thou raving? thou wast wont to have some sense; has the other sot frightened himself and thee too? speak, what is it he fancies he has seen?" "Why, my lord," replied Jaquez, trembling, "I was going to tell your highness, that since the calamitous misfortune of my young lord, God rest his precious soul! not one of us, your highness's faithful servants—indeed we are, my lord, though poor men—I say, not one of us has dared to set a foot about the castle, but two together: so, Diego and I, thinking that my young lady might be in the great gallery, went up there to look for her, and tell her your highness wanted something to impart to her." "O blundering fools!" cried Manfred, "and, in the mean time, she has made her escape, because you were afraid of goblins! Why, thou knave! she left me in the gallery; I came from thence myself." "For all that, she may be there still, for aught I know," said Jaquez, "but the devil shall have me before I seek her there again—poor Diego! I do not believe he will ever recover it!" "Recover what?" said Manfred; "am I never to learn what it is has terrified these rascals? but I lose my time: follow me, slave; I will see if she is in the gallery." "For heaven's sake, my dear good lord," cried Jaquez, "do not go to the gallery! Satan himself, I believe, is in the chamber next to the gallery." Manfred, who hitherto had treated the terror of his servants as an idle panic, was struck at this new circumstance. He recollected the apparition of the portrait, and the sudden closing of the door at the end of the gallery—his voice faltered, and he asked with disorder, "What is in the great chamber?" "My lord," said

Jaquez, "when Diego and I came into the gallery—he went first, for he said he had more courage thán I—So, when we came into the gallery, we found nobody. We looked under every bench and stool; and still we found nobody." "Were all the pictures in their places?" said Manfred. "Yes, my lord," answered Jaquez, "but we did not think of looking behind them." "Well, well," said Manfred, "proceed." "When we came to the door of the great chamber," continued Jaquez, "we found it shut." "And could not you open it?" said Manfred. "Oh yes, my lord; would to heaven we had not," replied he. "Nay, it was not I neither, it was Diego: he was grown fool-hardy, and would go on, though I advised him not—if ever I open a door that is shut again!" "Trifle not," said Manfred, shuddering, "but tell me what you saw in the great chamber, on opening the door." "I, my lord!" said Jaquez, "I saw nothing; I was behind Diego; but I heard the noise." "Jaquez," said Manfred, in a solemn tone of voice, "tell me, I adjure thee by the souls of my ancestors, what was it thou sawest? what was it thou heardest?" "It was Diego saw it, my lord, it was not I," replied Jaquez; "I only heard the noise. Diego had no sooner opened the door, than he cried out, and ran back—I ran back too, and said, 'Is it the ghost?' 'The ghost! no, no,' said Diego, and his hair stood on end—'It is a giant, I believe; he is all clad in armour, for I saw his foot and part of his leg, and they are as large as the helmet, below in the court.' As he said these words, my lord, we heard a violent motion, and the rattling of armour, as if the giant was rising; for Diego has told me since, that he believes the giant was lying down, for the foot and leg were stretched at length on the floor. Before we could get to the end of the gallery, we heard the door of the great chamber clap behind us, but we did not dare turn back to see if the giant was following us—yet, now I think on it, we must have heard him if he had pursued us. But, for heaven's sake, good my lord, send for the chaplain, and have the castle exorcised! for, for certain, it is enchanted." "Aye, pray do, my lord," cried all the servants at once, "or we must leave your highness's service." "Peace, dotards!" said Manfred, "and follow me; I will know what all this means."—"We, my lord!" cried they, with one voice, "we would not go up to the gallery for your highness's revenue." The young peasant, who had stood silent, now spoke. "Will your highness," said he, "permit me to try this adventure? my life is of consequence to nobody: I fear no bad angel, and have offended no good one." "Your behaviour is above your seeming;" said Manfred, viewing him with surprise and admiration—"hereafter I will reward your bravery—but now," continued he, with a sigh, "I am so circumstanced, that I dare trust no eyes but my own—however, I give you leave to accompany me."

Manfred, when he first followed Isabella from the gallery, had gone directly to the apartment of his wife, concluding the princess had retired thither. Hippolita, who knew his step, rose with anxious fondness to meet her lord, whom she had not seen since the death of their son. She would have flown in a transport, mixed of joy and grief, to his bosom; but he pushed her rudely off, and said, "Where is Isabella?"—"Isabella, my lord!" said the astonished Hippolita. "Yes! Isabella;" cried Manfred, imperiously; "I want Isabella."—"My lord," replied Matilda, who perceived how much his behaviour had shocked her mother, "she has not been with us since your highness summoned her to your apartment." "Tell me where she is," said the prince; "I do not want to know where she has been." "My good lord," said Hippolita, "your daughter tells you the truth: Isabella left us by your command, and has not returned since; but, my good lord, compose yourself; retire to your rest: this dismal day has disordered you. Isabella shall wait your orders in the morning." "What then, you know where she is!" cried Manfred: "Tell me directly, for I will not lose an instant—and you, woman," speaking to his wife, "order your chaplain to attend me forthwith." "Isabella," said Hippolita, calmly, "is retired, I suppose, to her chamber: she is not accustomed to watch at this late hour. Gracious my lord," continued she, "let me know what has disturbed you. Has Isabella offended you?" "Trouble me not with questions," said Manfred, "but tell me where she is." "Matilda shall call her," said the princess—"Sit down, my lord, and resume your wonted fortitude." "What! art thou jealous of Isabella," replied he, "that you wish to be present at our interview?" "Good heavens! my lord," said Hippolita, "what is it your highness means?"—"Thou wilt know ere many minutes are past," said the cruel prince. "Send your chaplain to me, and wait my pleasure here." At these words he flung out of the room in search of Isabella; leaving the amazed ladies thunderstruck with his words and frantic deportment, and lost in vain conjectures on what he was meditating.

Manfred was now returning from the vault, attended by the peasant, and a few of his servants, whom he had obliged to accompany him. He ascended the stair-case without stopping, till he arrived at the gallery, at the door of which he met Hippolita and her chaplain. When Diego had been dismissed by Manfred, he had gone directly to the princess's apartment with the alarm of what he had seen. That excellent lady, who no more than Manfred doubted of the reality of the vision, yet affected to treat it as a delirium of the servant. Willing, however, to save her lord from any additional shock, and prepared by a series of grief not to tremble at any accession to it, she determined to make herself the first sacrifice, if fate had marked the present hour for their destruction. Dismissing the reluctant Matilda to her rest, who in vain sued for leave to accompany her mother, and attended only by her chaplain, Hippolita had visited the gallery and great chamber; and now, with more serenity of soul than she had felt for many hours, she met her lord, and assured him that the vision of the gigantic leg and foot was all a fable; and, no doubt, an impression made by fear, and the dark and dismal hour of the night, on the minds of his servants. She and the chaplain had examined the chamber, and found everything in the usual order.

Manfred, though persuaded, like his wife, that the vision had been no work of fancy, recovered a little from the tempest of mind into which so many strange events had thrown him. Ashamed, too, of his inhuman treatment of a princess, who returned every injury with new marks of tenderness and duty; he felt returning love forcing itself into his eyes—but not less ashamed of feeling remorse towards one, against whom he was inwardly meditating a yet more bitter outrage, he curbed the yearnings of his heart, and did not dare to lean even towards pity. The next transition of his soul was to exquisite villainy. Presuming on the unshaken submission of Hippolita, he flattered himself that she would not only acquiesce with patience to a divorce, but would obey, if it was his pleasure, in endeavouring to persuade Isabella to give him her hand; but, ere he could indulge this horrid hope, he reflected that Isabella was not to be found. Coming to himself, he gave orders that every avenue to the castle should be strictly guarded, and charged his domestics, on pain of their lives, to suffer nobody to pass out. The young peasant, to whom he spoke favourably, he ordered to remain in a small chamber on the stairs, in which there was a pallet-bed, and the key of which he took away himself, telling the youth he would talk with him in the morning. Then, dismissing his attendants, and bestowing a sullen kind of half-nod on Hippolita, he retired to his own chamber.

CHAPTER II

Matilda, who, by Hippolita's order, had retired to her apartment, was ill-disposed to take any rest. The shocking fate of her brother had deeply affected her. She was surprised at not seeing Isabella; but the strange words which had fallen from her father, and his obscure menace to the princess, his wife, accompanied by the most furious behaviour, had filled her gentle mind with terror and alarm. She waited anxiously for the return of Bianca, a young damsel that attended her, whom she had sent to learn what was become of Isabella. Bianca soon appeared, and informed her mistress of what she had gathered from the servants, that Isabella was nowhere to be found. She related the adventure of the young peasant, who had been discovered in the vault, though with many simple additions from the incoherent account of the domestics; and she dwelled principally on the gigantic leg and foot, which had been seen in the gallery chamber. This last circumstance had terrified Bianca so much, that she was rejoiced when Matilda told her that she should not go to rest, but would watch till the princess should rise.

The young princess wearied herself in conjectures on the flight of Isabella, and on the threats of Manfred to her mother. "But what business could he have so urgent with the chaplain," said Matilda; "does he intend to have my brother's body interred privately in the chapel?" "Oh! madam," said Bianca, "now I guess. As you are become his heiress, he is impatient to have you married; he has always been raving for more sons; I warrant he is now impatient for grandsons. As sure as I live, madam, I shall see you a bride at last—Good madam, you won't cast off your faithful Bianca! you won't put Donna Rosara over me, now you are a great princess!" "My poor Bianca," said Matilda, "how fast your thoughts amble! I a great princess! What hast thou seen in Manfred's behaviour, since my brother's death, that bespeaks any increase of tenderness to me—but he is my father, and I must not complain. Nay, if heaven shuts my father's heart against me, it over-pays my little merit in the tenderness of my mother. O that dear mother! yes, Bianca, 'tis there I feel the rugged temper of Manfred. I can support his harshness to me with patience; but it wounds my soul when I am witness to his causeless severity towards her." "Oh! madam," said Bianca, "all men use their wives so, when they are weary of them." "And yet you congratulated me but now," said Matilda, "when you fancied my father intended to dispose of me!" "I would have you a great lady," replied Bianca, "come what will. I do not wish to see you moped in a convent, as you would be if you had your will, and if my lady, your mother, who knows that a bad husband is better than no husband at all, did not hinder you—Bless me! what noise is that! St. Nicholas forgive me! I was but in jest." "It is the wind," said Matilda, "whistling through the battlements in the tower above: you have heard it a thousand times." "Nay," said Bianca, "there was no harm in what I said: it is no sin to talk of matrimony—and so, madam, as I was saying, if my lord Manfred should offer you a handsome young prince for a bridegroom, you would drop him a curtsey, and tell him you would rather take the veil?" "Thank heaven! I am in no such danger," said Matilda: "you know how many proposals for me he has rejected." "And you thank him, like a dutiful daughter, do you, madam? but come, madam; suppose, tomorrow morning, he was to send for you to the great council chamber, and there you should find at his elbow a lovely young prince, with large black eyes, a smooth white forehead, and manly curling locks like jet; in short, madam, a young hero resembling the picture of the good Alfonso in the gallery, which you sit and gaze at for hours together." "Do not speak lightly of that picture," interrupted Matilda, sighing: "I know the adoration, with which I look at that picture, is uncommon—but I am not in love with a coloured panel. The character of that virtuous prince, the veneration with which my mother has inspired me for his memory, the orisons which, I know not why, she has enjoined me to pour forth at his tomb, all have concurred to persuade me, that, somehow or other, my destiny is linked with something relating to him." "Lord! madam, how should that be?" said Bianca; "I have always heard that your family was no way related to his; and I am sure I cannot conceive why my lady, the princess, sends you in a cold morning, or a damp evening, to pray at his tomb: he is no saint by the almanack. If you must pray, why does she not bid you address yourself to our great St. Nicholas? I am sure he is the saint I pray to for a husband."—"Perhaps my mind would be less affected," said Matilda, "if my mother would explain her reasons to me: but it is the mystery she observes, that inspires me with this—I know not what to call it. As she never acts from caprice, I am sure there is some fatal secret at bottom—nay, I know there is: in her agony of grief for my brother's death she dropped some words that intimated as much." "Oh! dear madam," cried Bianca, "what were they?" "No," said Matilda; "if a parent lets fall a word, and wishes it recalled, it is not for a child to utter it." "What! was she sorry for what she had said?" asked Bianca; "I am sure, madam, you may trust me." "With my own little secrets, when I have any, I may," said Matilda; "but never with my mother's: a child ought to have no ears or eyes, but as a parent directs." "Well, to be sure, madam, you was born to be a saint," said Bianca, "and there is no resisting one's vocation: you will end in a convent at last. But there is my lady Isabella would not be so reserved to me; she will let me talk to her of young men; and when a handsome cavalier has come to the castle, she has owned to me that she wished your brother Conrad resembled him." "Bianca," said the princess, "I do not allow you to mention my friend disrespectfully. Isabella is of a cheerful disposition, but her soul is as pure as virtue itself. She knows your idle babbling humour, and perhaps has now and then encouraged it, to divert melancholy, and enliven the solitude in which my father keeps us."—"Blessed Mary!" said Bianca, starting, "there it is again! dear madam, do you hear nothing? this castle is certainly haunted!"—"Peace!" said Matilda, "and listen! I did think I heard a voice—but it must be fancy; your terrors, I suppose, have infected me." "Indeed! indeed! madam," said Bianca, half weeping with agony, "I am sure I heard a voice!" "Does anybody lie in the chamber beneath?" said the princess. "Nobody has dared to lie there," answered Bianca, "since the great astrologer, that was your brother's tutor, drowned himself. For certain, madam, his ghost and the young prince's are now met in the chamber below—for heaven's sake let us fly to your mother's apartment!" "I charge you not to stir," said Matilda; "if they are spirits in pain, we may ease their sufferings by questioning them. They can mean no hurt to us, for we have not injured them; and

if they should, shall we be more safe in one chamber than another? reach me my beads; we will say a prayer, and then speak to
them." "Oh! dear lady, I would not speak to a ghost for the
world!" cried Bianca. As she said these words, they heard the casement of the little chamber, below Matilda's, open. They listened
attentively, and in a few minutes thought they heard a person
sing, but could not distinguish the words. "This can be no evil
spirit," said the princess, in a low voice: "it is undoubtedly one
of the family—open the window, and we shall know the voice."
"I dare not indeed, madam," said Bianca. "Thou art a very fool,"
said Matilda, opening the window gently herself. The noise the
princess made was, however, heard by the person beneath, who
stopped; and they concluded had heard the casement open. "Is
anybody below?" said the princess: "if there is, speak." "Yes," said
an unknown voice. "Who is it?" said Matilda. "A stranger," replied the voice. "What stranger?" said she; "and how didst thou
come here at this unusual hour, when all the gates of the castle
are locked?" "I am not here willingly," answered the voice—"but
pardon me, lady, if I have disturbed your rest: I knew not that I
was overheard. Sleep had forsaken me; I left a restless couch, and
came to waste the irksome hours with gazing on the fair approach
of morning, impatient to be dismissed from this castle." "Thy
words and accents," said Matilda, "are of a melancholy cast: if
thou art unhappy, I pity thee. If poverty afflicts thee, let me know
it: I will mention thee to the princess, whose beneficent soul ever
melts for the distressed; and she will relieve thee." "I am indeed
unhappy," said the stranger, "and I know not what wealth is: but
I do not complain of the lot which heaven has cast for me: I am
young and healthy, and am not ashamed of owing my support to
myself—yet think me not proud, or that I disdain your generous
offers! I will remember you in my orisons, and I will pray for
blessings on your gracious self and your noble mistress. If I sigh,
lady, it is for others, not for myself." "Now I have it, madam!"
said Bianca, whispering the princess; "this is certainly the young
peasant; and, by my conscience, he is in love—well this is a charming adventure!—do, madam, let us sift him. He does not know you,
but takes you for one of my lady Hippolita's women." "Art thou
not ashamed, Bianca!" said the princess: "what right have we
to pry into the secrets of this young man's heart? he seems virtuous and frank, and tells us he is unhappy: are those circumstances

that authorise us to make a property of him? how are we entitled to his confidence?" "Lord! madam, how little you know of love!" replied Bianca: "why lovers have no pleasure equal to talking of their mistress!" "And would you have me become a peasant's confidant?" said the princess. "Well, then, let me talk to him," said Bianca: "though I have the honour of being your highness's maid of honour, I was not always so great: besides, if love levels ranks, it raises them too: I have a respect for a young man in love." "Peace, simpleton!" said the princess; "though he said he was unhappy, it does not follow that he must be in love. Think of all that has happened to-day, and tell me, if there are no misfortunes but what love causes!—Stranger," resumed the princess, "if thy misfortunes have not been occasioned by thy own fault, and are within the compass of the princess Hippolita's power to redress, I will take upon me to answer that she will be thy protectress. When thou art dismissed from this castle, repair to holy father Jerome, at the convent adjoining to the church of St. Nicholas, and make thy story known to him, as far as thou thinkest meet: he will not fail to inform the princess, who is the mother of all that want her assistance. Farewell: it is not seemly for me to hold farther converse with a man, at this unwonted hour." "May the saints guard thee, gracious lady!" replied the peasant—"but oh! if a poor and worthless stranger might presume to beg a minute's audience farther—am I so happy? the casement is not shut—might I venture to ask"—"Speak quickly," said Matilda; "the morning dawns apace; should the labourers come into the fields and perceive us —what wouldst thou ask?" "I know not how—I know not if I dare," said the young stranger, faltering, "yet the humanity with which you have spoken to me emboldens—lady! dare I trust you?" "Heavens!" said Matilda, "What dost thou mean? with what wouldst thou trust me? speak boldly, if thy secret is fit to be entrusted to a virtuous breast." "I would ask," said the peasant, recollecting himself, "whether what I have heard from the domestics is true, that the princess is missing from the castle?" "What imports it to thee to know?" replied Matilda. "Thy first words bespoke a prudent and becoming gravity. Dost thou come hither to pry into the secrets of Manfred? Adieu. I have been mistaken in thee." Saying these words, she shut the casement hastily, without giving the young man time to reply. "I had acted more wisely," said the princess to Bianca, with some sharpness, "if I had let thee converse with this peasant: his inquisitiveness seems of a piece with thy own." "It is not fit for me to argue with your highness," replied Bianca; "but perhaps the questions, I should have put to him, would have been more to the purpose than those you have been pleased to ask him." "Oh! no doubt;" said Matilda: "you are a very discreet personage! may I know what you would have asked him?" "A by-stander often sees more of the game than those that play," answered Bianca. "Does your highness think, madam, that his question about my Lady Isabella was the result of mere curiosity? No, no, madam; there is more in it than you great folks are aware of. Lopez told me, that all the servants believe this young fellow contrived my Lady Isabella's escape: now, pray, madam, observe—you and I both know that my Lady Isabella never much fancied the prince your brother—well! he is killed just in the critical minute—I accuse nobody. A helmet falls from the moon—so my lord, your father, says; but Lopez and all the servants say, that this young spark is a magician, and stole it from Alfonso's tomb." "Have done with this rhapsody of impertinence," said Matilda. "Nay, madam, as you please," cried Bianca; "yet it is very particular, though, that my Lady Isabella should be missing the very same day, and that this young sorcerer should be found at the mouth of the trap-door; I accuse nobody; but if my young lord came honestly by his death"—"Dare not, on thy duty," said Matilda, "to breathe a suspicion on the purity of my dear Isabella's fame." "Purity or not purity," said Bianca, "gone she is— a stranger is found that nobody knows: you question him yourself: he tells you he is in love, or unhappy, it is the same thing— nay, he owned he was unhappy about others; and is anybody unhappy about another, unless they are in love with them? And at the very next word, he asks innocently, poor soul! if my Lady Isabella is missing." "To be sure," said Matilda, "thy observations are not totally without foundation—Isabella's flight amazes me: the curiosity of this stranger is very particular—yet Isabella never concealed a thought from me." "So she told you," said Bianca, "to fish out your secrets; but who knows, madam, but this stranger may be some prince in disguise? do, madam, let me open the window, and ask him a few questions!" "No," replied Matilda, "I will ask him myself: if he knows aught of Isabella, he is not worthy that I should converse farther with him." She was going to open the casement, when they heard the bell ring at the postern gate of the castle, which is on the right hand of the tower, where Matilda lay. This prevented the princess from renewing the conversation with the stranger.

After continuing silent for some time, "I am persuaded," said she to Bianca, "that whatever be the cause of Isabella's flight, it had no unworthy motive. If this stranger was accessary to it, she must be satisfied of his fidelity and worth. I observed, did not you, Bianca? that his words were tinctured with an uncommon infusion of piety. It was no ruffian's speech: his phrases were becoming a man of gentle birth." "I told you, madam," said Bianca, "that I was sure he was some prince in disguise." "Yet," said Matilda, "if he was privy to her escape, how will you account for his not accompanying her in her flight? why expose himself unnecessarily and rashly to my father's resentment?" "As for that, madam," replied she, "if he could get from under the helmet, he will find ways of eluding your father's anger. I do not doubt but he has some talisman or other about him." "You resolve everything into magic," said Matilda; "but a man, who has any intercourse with infernal spirits, does not dare to make use of those tremendous and holy words, which he uttered. Didst thou not observe with what fervour he vowed to remember me to heaven in his prayers? yes; Isabella was undoubtedly convinced of his piety." "Commend me to the piety of a young fellow and a damsel, that consult to elope!" said Bianca. "No, no, madam: my Lady Isabella is of another-guess mould than you take her for. She used indeed to sigh and lift up her eyes in your company, because she knows you are a saint—but when your back was turned"—"You wrong her," said Matilda: "Isabella is no hypocrite: she has a due sense of devotion, but never affected a call she has not. On the contrary, she always combated my inclination for the cloister; and, though I own the mystery she has made to me of her flight, confounds me; though it seems inconsistent with the friendship between us; I cannot forget the disinterested warmth with which she always opposed my taking the veil: she wished to see me married, though my dower would have been a loss to her and my brother's children. For her sake I will believe well of this young peasant." "Then you do think there is some liking between them?" said Bianca. While she was speaking, a servant came hastily into the chamber, and told the princess that the Lady Isabella was found. "Where?" said Matilda. "She has taken sanctuary in St. Nicholas's church," replied the servant: "father Jerome has brought the news himself: he is below with his highness." "Where is my mother?" said Matilda. "She is in her own chamber, madam, and has asked for you."

Manfred had risen at the first dawn of light, and gone to Hippolita's apartment, to enquire if she knew aught of Isabella. While he was questioning her, word was brought that Jerome demanded to speak with him. Manfred, little suspecting the cause of the friar's arrival, and knowing he was employed by Hippolita in her charities, ordered him to be admitted, intending to leave them together, while he pursued his search after Isabella. "Is your business with me or the princess?" said Manfred. "With both," replied the holy man. "The Lady Isabella"—"What of her?" interrupted Manfred, eagerly: "Is at St. Nicholas's altar," replied Jerome. "That is no business of Hippolita!" said Manfred, with confusion: "let us retire to my chamber, father; and inform me how she came thither." "No, my lord," replied the good man, with an air of firmness and authority, that daunted even the resolute Manfred, who could not help revering the saint-like virtues of Jerome—"my commission is to both; and, with your highness's good liking, in the presence of both I shall deliver it— but first, my lord, I must interrogate the princess, whether she is acquainted with the cause of the Lady Isabella's retirement from your castle." "No, on my soul;" said Hippolita; "does Isabella charge me with being privy to it?"—"Father," interrupted Manfred, "I pay due reverence to your holy profession; but I am sovereign here, and will allow no meddling priest to interfere in the affairs of my domestic. If you have aught to say, attend me to my chamber—I do not use to let my wife be acquainted with the secret affairs of my state; they are not within a woman's province." "My lord," said the holy man, "I am no intruder into the secrets of families. My office is to promote peace, to heal divisions, to preach repentance, and teach mankind to curb their headstrong passions. I forgive your highness's uncharitable apostrophe: I know my duty, and am the minister of a mightier prince than Manfred. Hearken to him, who speaks through my organs." Manfred trembled with rage and shame. Hippolita's countenance declared her astonishment and impatience, to know where this would end: her silence more strongly spoke her observance of Manfred.

"The Lady Isabella," resumed Jerome, "commends herself to both your highnesses; she thanks both for the kindness with which she has been treated in your castle: she deplores the loss of your son, and her own misfortune in not becoming the daughter of such wise and noble princes, whom she shall always respect as parents; she prays for uninterrupted union and felicity between you: (Manfred's colour changed) but, as it is no longer possible to be allied to you, she entreats your consent to remain in sanctuary, till she can learn news of her father; or, by the certainty of his death, be at liberty, with the approbation of her guardians, to dispose of herself in suitable marriage." "I shall give no such consent," said the prince; "but insist on her return to the castle without delay: I am answerable for her person to her guardians, and will not brook her being in any hands but my own." "Your highness will recollect whether that can any longer be proper," replied the friar. "I want no monitor," said Manfred, colouring; "Isabella's conduct leaves room for strange suspicions—and that young villain, who was at least the accomplice of her flight, if not the cause of it"—"The cause!" interrupted Jerome; "was a young man the cause?"—"This is not to be borne!" cried Manfred. "Am I to be bearded in my own palace by an insolent monk? thou art privy, I guess, to their amours."—"I would pray to heaven to clear up your uncharitable surmises," said Jerome, "if your highness were not satisfied in your conscience how unjustly you accuse me. I do pray to heaven to pardon that uncharitableness: and I implore your highness to leave the princess at peace in that holy place, where she is not liable to be disturbed by such vain and worldly fantasies as discourses of love from any man." "Cant not to me," said Manfred, "but return and bring the princess to her duty." "It is my duty to prevent her return hither;" said Jerome. "She is where orphans and virgins are safest from the snares and wiles of this world; and nothing but a parent's authority shall take her thence." "I am her parent," cried Manfred, "and demand her." "She wished to have you for her parent," said the friar: "but heaven that forbade that connection, has for ever dissolved all ties betwixt you: and I announce to your highness"—"Stop! audacious man," said Manfred, "and dread my displeasure." "Holy father," said Hippolita, "it is your office to be no respecter of persons: you must speak as your duty prescribes—but it is my duty to hear nothing that it pleases not my lord I should

hear. Attend the prince to his chamber. I will retire to my oratory,
and pray the blessed virgin to inspire you with her holy counsels,
and to restore the heart of my gracious lord to its wonted peace
and gentleness." "Excellent woman!" said the friar. "My lord, I
attend your pleasure."

Manfred, accompanied by the friar, passed to his own apartment, where, shutting the door, "I perceive, father," said he, "that
Isabella has acquainted you with my purpose. Now, hear my resolve, and obey. Reasons of state, most urgent reasons, my own
and the safety of my people, demand that I should have a son. It
is in vain to expect an heir from Hippolita. I have made choice of
Isabella. You must bring her back; and you must do more. I know
the influence you have with Hippolita: her conscience is in your
hands. She is, I allow, a faultless woman: her soul is set on heaven,
and scorns the little grandeur of this world: you can withdraw her
from it entirely. Persuade her to consent to the dissolution of our
marriage, and to retire into a monastery: she shall endow one if
she will: and shall have the means of being as liberal to your order, as she or you can wish. Thus you will divert the calamities
that are hanging over our heads, and have the merit of saving the
principality of Otranto from destruction. You are a prudent man;
and, though the warmth of my temper betrayed me into some un-
becoming expressions, I honour your virtue, and wish to be indebted to you for the repose of my life and the preservation of
my family."

"The will of heaven be done!" said the friar. "I am but its
worthless instrument. It makes use of my tongue, to tell thee,
prince, of thy unwarrantable designs. The injuries of the virtuous
Hippolita have mounted to the throne of pity. By me thou art
reprimanded for thy adulterous intention of repudiating her: by
me thou art warned not to pursue thine incestuous design on thy
contracted daughter. Heaven, that delivered her from thy fury,
when the judgments, so recently fallen on thy house, ought to have
inspired thee with other thoughts, will continue to watch over
her. Even I, a poor and despised friar, am able to protect her
from thy violence. I, sinner as I am, and uncharitably reviled by
your highness, as an accomplice of I know not what amours, scorn
the allurements with which it has pleased thee to tempt my honesty. I love my order; I honour devout souls; I respect the piety of
thy princess; but will not betray the confidence she reposes in me,

nor serve even the cause of religion by foul and sinful compliances; but, forsooth! the welfare of the state depends on your highness having a son! Heaven mocks the shortsighted views of man. But yester-morn, whose house was so great, so flourishing as Manfred's? Where is young Conrad now! My lord, I respect your tears, but I mean not to check them: let them flow, prince: they will weigh more with heaven, toward the welfare of thy subjects, than a marriage, which, founded on lust or policy, could never prosper. The sceptre, which passed from the race of Alfonso to thine, cannot be preserved by a match which the church will never allow. If it is the will of the Most High that Manfred's name must perish, resign yourself, my lord, to its decrees: and thus deserve a crown that can never pass away. Come, my lord; I like this sorrow; let us return to the princess: she is not apprised of your cruel intentions; nor did I mean more than to alarm you. You saw with what gentle patience, with what efforts of love, she heard, she rejected hearing the extent of your guilt. I know she longs to fold you in her arms, and assure you of her unalterable affection." "Father," said the prince, "you mistake my compunction: true; I honour Hippolita's virtues; I think her a saint; and wish it were for my soul's health to tie faster the knot that has united us—but alas! father, you know not the bitterest of my pangs. It is some time that I have had scruples on the legality of our union: Hippolita is related to me in the fourth degree. It is true, we had a dispensation; but I have been informed that she had also been contracted to another. This it is that sits heavy at my heart: to this state of unlawful wedlock I impute the visitation that has fallen on me in the death of Conrad! Ease my conscience of this burden: dissolve our marriage, and accomplish the work of godliness which your divine exhortations have commenced in my soul."

How cutting was the anguish which the good man felt, when he perceived this turn in the wily prince! He trembled for Hippolita, whose ruin he saw was determined; and he feared if Manfred had no hope of recovering Isabella, that his impatience for a son would direct him to some other object, who might not be equally proof against the temptation of Manfred's rank. For some time the holy man remained absorbed in thought. At length, conceiving some hopes from delay, he thought the wisest conduct would be to prevent the prince from despairing of recovering Isabella. Her, the friar knew he could dispose, from her affection to Hippolita, and from the aversion she had expressed to him for Manfred's addresses, to second his views, till the censures of the church could be fulminated against a divorce. With this intention, as if struck with the prince's scruples, he at length said; "My lord, I have been pondering on what your highness has said: and if, in truth, it is delicacy of conscience that is the real motive of your repugnance to your virtuous lady, far be it from me to endeavour to harden your heart. The church is an indulgent mother: unfold your griefs to her: she alone can administer comfort to your soul, either by satisfying your conscience, or, upon examination of your scruples, by setting you at liberty, and indulging you in the lawful means of continuing your lineage. In the latter case, if the Lady Isabella can be brought to consent"—Manfred, who concluded that he had either overreached the good man, or that his first warmth had been but a tribute paid to appearance, was overjoyed at his sudden turn, and repeated the most magnificent promises, if he should succeed by the friar's mediation. The well-meaning priest suffered him to deceive himself, fully determined to traverse his views, instead of seconding them.

"Since we now understand one another," resumed the prince, "I expect, father, that you satisfy me in one point. Who is the youth that I found in the vault? He must have been privy to Isabella's flight; tell me truly; is he her lover? or is he an agent for another's passion? I have often suspected Isabella's indifference to my son: a thousand circumstances crowd on my mind that confirm that suspicion. She herself was so conscious of it, that, while I discoursed with her, in the gallery, she outran my suspicions, and endeavoured to justify herself from coolness to Conrad." The friar, who knew nothing of the youth, but what he had learnt occasionally from the princess, ignorant what was become of him, and not sufficiently reflecting on the impetuosity of Manfred's temper, conceived that it might not be amiss to sow the seeds of jealousy in his mind: they might be turned to some use hereafter, either by prejudicing the prince against Isabella, if he persisted in that union; or, by diverting his attention to a wrong scent, and employing his thoughts on a visionary intrigue, prevent his engaging in any new pursuit. With this unhappy policy, he answered in a manner to confirm Manfred in the belief of some connection between Isabella and the youth.

The prince, whose passions wanted little fuel to throw them

into a blaze, fell into a rage at the idea of what the friar had suggested. "I will fathom to the bottom of this intrigue," cried he; and quitting Jerome abruptly, with a command to remain there till his return, he hastened to the great hall of the castle, and ordered the peasant to be brought before him. "Thou hardened young impostor!" said the prince, as soon as he saw the youth; "what becomes of thy boasted veracity now? it was Providence, was it, and the light of the moon, that discovered the lock of the trap-door to thee? Tell me, audacious boy, who thou art, and how long thou hast been acquainted with the princess—and take care to answer with less equivocation than thou didst last night, or tortures shall wring the truth from thee." The young man, perceiving that his share in the flight of the princess was discovered, and concluding that anything he should say, could no longer be of service or detriment to her, replied, "I am no impostor, my lord, nor have I deserved opprobrious language. I answered to every question, your highness put to me last night, with the same veracity that I shall speak now; and that will not be from fear of your tortures, but because my soul abhors a falsehood. Please to repeat your questions, my lord; I am ready to give you all the satisfaction in my power." "You know my questions," replied the prince, "and only want time to prepare an evasion. Speak directly; who art thou? and how long hast thou been known to the princess?" "I am a labourer at the next village," said the peasant; "my name is Theodore. The princess found me in the vault last night; before that hour I never was in her presence." "I may believe as much, or as little as I please of this," said Manfred; "but I will hear thy own story, before I examine into the truth of it. Tell me what reason did the princess give thee for making her escape? thy life depends on thy answer." "She told me," replied Theodore, "that she was on the brink of destruction, and that if she could not escape from the castle, she was in danger, in a few moments, of being made miserable for ever." "And on this slight foundation, on a silly girl's report," said Manfred, "thou didst hazard my displeasure?" "I fear no man's displeasure," said Theodore, "when a woman in distress puts herself under my protection." During this examination, Matilda was going to the apartment of Hippolita. At the upper end of the hall, where Manfred sat, was a boarded gallery with latticed windows, through which Matilda and Bianca were to pass. Hearing her father's voice, and seeing the servants

assembled round him, she stopped to learn the occasion. The prisoner soon drew her attention; the steady and composed manner in which he answered, and the gallantry of his last reply,
which were the first words she heard distinctly, interested her in
his favour. His person was noble, handsome, and commanding,
even in that situation; but his countenance soon engrossed her
whole care. "Heavens! Bianca!" said the princess softly, "do I
dream? or is not that youth the exact resemblance of Alfonso's
picture in the gallery?" She could say no more, for her father's
voice grew louder at every word. "This bravado," said he, "sur-
passes all thy former insolence. Thou shalt experience the wrath
with which thou darest to trifle. Seize him," continued Manfred,
"and bind him: the first news the princess hears of her champion
shall be, that he has lost his head for her sake." "The injustice of
which thou art guilty towards me," said Theodore, "convinces me
that I have done a good deed, in delivering the princess from thy
tyranny. May she be happy, whatever becomes of me!" "This is a
lover!" cried Manfred in a rage: "a peasant within sight of death
is not animated by such sentiments. Tell me, tell me, rash boy,
who thou art, or the rack shall force thy secret from thee." "Thou
hast threatened me with death already," saith the youth, "for the
truth I have told thee: if that is all the encouragement I am to expect for sincerity, I am not tempted to indulge thy vain curiosity
farther." "Then thou wilt not speak?" said Manfred. "I will not,"
replied he. "Bear him away into the court-yard," said Manfred: "I
will see his head this instant severed from his body." Matilda
fainted at hearing these words. Bianca shrieked, and cried,
"Help! help! the princess is dead!" Manfred started at this ejacu-
lation, and demanded what was the matter? The young peasant,
who heard it too, was struck with horror, and asked eagerly the
same question; but Manfred ordered him to be hurried into
the court, and kept there for execution, till he had informed himself of the cause of Bianca's shrieks. When he learned the meaning, he treated it as a womanish panic, and ordering Matilda to be
carried to her apartment, he rushed into the court, and calling for
one of his guards, bade Theodore kneel down and prepare to receive the fatal blow.

The undaunted youth received the bitter sentence with a resignation that touched every heart but Manfred's. He wished earnestly to know the meaning of the words he had heard relating to

the princess; but fearing to exasperate the tyrant more against her, he desisted. The only boon he deigned to ask, was, that he might be permitted to have a confessor, and make his peace with heaven. Manfred, who hoped, by the confessor's means, to come at the youth's history, readily granted his request: and being convinced that father Jerome was now in his interest, he ordered him to be called and shrieve the prisoner. The holy man, who had little foreseen the catastrophe that his imprudence occasioned, fell on his knees to the prince, and adjured him, in the most solemn manner, not to shed innocent blood. He accused himself, in the bitterest terms, for his indiscretion, endeavoured to exculpate the youth, and left no method untried to soften the tyrant's rage.

Manfred, more incensed than appeased by Jerome's intercession, whose retraction now made him suspect he had been imposed upon by both, commanded the friar to do his duty, telling him he would not allow the prisoner many minutes for confession. "Nor do I ask many, my lord;" said the unhappy young man. "My sins, thank heaven! have not been numerous; nor exceed what might be expected at my years. Dry your tears, good father, and let us dispatch: this is a bad world; nor have I had cause to leave it with regret." "Oh! wretched youth!" said Jerome; "how canst thou bear the sight of me with patience? I am thy murderer! it is I have brought this dismal hour upon thee." "I forgive thee from my soul," said the youth, "as I hope heaven will pardon me. Hear my confession, father; and give me thy blessing." "How can I prepare thee for thy passage, as I ought?" said Jerome. "Thou canst not be saved without pardoning thy foes—and canst thou forgive that impious man there?" "I can," said Theodore; "I do." "And does not this touch thee? cruel prince!" said the friar. "I sent for thee to confess him," said Manfred sternly; "not to plead for him. Thou didst first incense me against him; his blood be upon thy head!" "It will! it will!" said the good man, in an agony of sorrow. "Thou and I must never hope to go where this blessed youth is going!" "Dispatch!" said Manfred: "I am no more to be moved by the whining of priests, than by the shrieks of women." "What!" said the youth; "is it possible that my fate could have occasioned what I heard! is the princess then again in thy power?" "Thou dost but remember me of my wrath," said Manfred: "prepare thee, for this moment is thy last." The youth, who felt his indignation rise, and who was touched with the sorrow which he saw he had infused into all the spectators, as well as into the friar, suppressed his emotions, and putting off his doublet, and unbuttoning his collar, knelt down to his prayers. As he stooped, his shirt slipped down below his shoulder, and discovered the mark of a bloody arrow. "Gracious heaven!" cried the holy man, starting, "what do I see! It is my child! my Theodore!"

The passions that ensued, must be conceived; they cannot be painted. The tears of the assistants were suspended by wonder, rather than stopped by joy. They seemed to inquire into the eyes of their lord what they ought to feel. Surprise, doubt, tenderness, respect, succeeded each other in the countenance of the youth. He received, with modest submission, the effusion of the old man's tears and embraces; yet, afraid of giving a loose to hope, and suspecting, from what had passed, the inflexibility of Manfred's temper, he cast a glance towards the prince, as if to say, canst thou be unmoved at such a scene as this?

Manfred's heart was capable of being touched. He forgot his anger in his astonishment; yet his pride forbade his owning himself affected. He even doubted whether this discovery was not a contrivance of the friar to save the youth. "What may this mean?" said he: "how can he be thy son? is it consistent with thy profession, or reputed sanctity, to avow a peasant's offspring for the fruit of thy irregular amours?" "Oh! God," said the holy man, "dost thou question his being mine? could I feel the anguish I do, if I were not his father? Spare him! good prince, spare him! and revile me as thou pleasest." "Spare him! spare him!" cried the attendants, "for this good man's sake!" "Peace!" said Manfred, sternly: "I must know more, ere I am disposed to pardon. A saint's bastard may be no saint himself." "Injurious lord!" said Theodore; "add not insult to cruelty. If I am this venerable man's son, though no prince, as thou art, know, the blood that flows in my veins"—"Yes," said the friar, interrupting him, "his blood is noble; nor is he that abject thing, my lord, you speak him. He is my lawful son; and Sicily can boast of few houses more ancient than that of Falconara—but alas, my lord, what is blood! what is nobility! we are all reptiles, miserable, sinful creatures. It is piety alone that can distinguish us from the dust whence we sprung, and whither we must return." "Truce to your sermon," said Manfred; "you forget, you are no longer friar Jerome, but the Count of Falconara. Let me know your history; you will have time enough to moralize hereafter, if you should not happen to obtain the grace of that sturdy criminal there." "Mother of God!" said the friar, "is it possible my lord can refuse a father the life of his only, his long-lost child! Trample me, my lord, scorn, afflict me, accept my life for his, but spare my son!" "Thou canst feel then," said Manfred, "what it is to lose an only son! a little hour ago, thou didst preach up resignation to me: my house, if fate so pleased, must perish—but the Count of Falconara"—"Alas! my lord," said Jerome, "I confess I have offended; but aggravate not an old man's sufferings! I boast not of my family, nor think of such vanities: it is nature that pleads for this boy; it is the memory of the dear woman that bore him. Is she, Theodore, is she dead?" "Her soul has long been with the blessed," said Theodore. "Oh! how?" cried Jerome, "tell me—no—she is happy! Thou art all my care now! Most dread lord! will you—will you grant me my poor boy's life?" "Return to thy convent," answered Manfred; "conduct the princess hither; obey me in what else thou knowest; and I promise thee the life of thy son." "Oh! my lord," said Jerome, "is my honesty the price I must pay for this dear youth's safety?" "For me!" cried Theodore: "let me die a thousand deaths, rather than stain thy conscience. What is it the tyrant would exact of thee? is the princess still safe from his power? protect her, thou venerable old man; and let all the weight of his wrath fall on me." Jerome endeavoured to check the impetuosity of the youth; and ere Manfred could reply, the trampling of horses was heard, and a brazen trumpet, which hung without the gate of the castle, was suddenly sounded. At the same instant, the sable plumes on the enchanted helmet, which still remained at the other end of the court, were tempestuously agitated, and nodded thrice, as if bowed by some invisible wearer.

CHAPTER III

Manfred's heart misgave him, when he beheld the plumage on the miraculous casque shaken in concert with the sounding of the brazen trumpet. "Father!" said he to Jerome, whom he now ceased to treat as Count of Falconara, "what mean these portents? If I have offended"—the plumes were shaken with greater violence

than before. "Unhappy prince that I am!" cried Manfred: "Holy
father! will you not assist me with your prayers?" "My lord," replied Jerome, "heaven is no doubt displeased with your mockery
of its servants. Submit yourself to the church; and cease to perse-
cute her ministers. Dismiss this innocent youth; and learn to respect the holy character I wear: heaven will not be trifled with:
you see"—the trumpet sounded again. "I acknowledge I have
been too hasty," said Manfred. "Father, do you go to the wicket,
and demand who is at the gate." "Do you grant me the life of
Theodore?" replied the friar. "I do," said Manfred; "but inquire
who is without!"

Jerome, falling on the neck of his son, discharged a flood of
tears that spoke the fulness of his soul. "You promised to go to the
gate," said Manfred. "I thought," replied the friar, "your highness
would excuse my thanking you first in this tribute of my heart."
"Go, dearest sir," said Theodore; "obey the prince—I do not
deserve that you should delay his satisfaction for me."

Jerome, inquiring who was without, was answered, a herald.
"From whom?" said he. "From the knight of the gigantic sabre";
said the herald; "and I must speak with the usurper of Otranto."
Jerome returned to the prince, and did not fail to repeat the message, in the very words it had been uttered. The first sounds struck
Manfred with terror; but when he heard himself stiled usurper,
his rage re-kindled, and all his courage revived. "Usurper! insolent villain!" cried he, "who dares to question my title? Retire,
father; this is no business for monks: I will meet this presumptuous man myself. Go to your convent, and prepare the princess's
return: your son shall be a hostage for your fidelity: his life depends on your obedience." "Good heaven! my lord," cried Jerome, "your highness did but this instant freely pardon my child
—have you so soon forgot the interposition of heaven?" "Heaven,"
replied Manfred, "does not send heralds to question the title of
a lawful prince; I doubt whether it even notifies its will through
friars—but that is your affair, not mine. At present you know
my pleasure; and it is not a saucy herald that shall save your son,
if you do not return with the princess."

It was in vain for the holy man to reply. Manfred commanded
him to be conducted to the postern gate, and shut out from the
castle: and he ordered some of his attendants to carry Theodore
to the top of the black tower, and guard him strictly; scarce per-

mitting the father and son to exchange a hasty embrace at parting. He then withdrew to the hall, and, seating himself in princely state, ordered the herald to be admitted to his presence.

"Well! thou insolent!" said the prince, "what wouldst thou with me?" "I come," replied he, "to thee, Manfred, usurper of the principality of Otranto, from the renowned and invincible knight, the knight of the gigantic sabre: in the name of his lord, Frederic Marquis of Vicenza, he demands the Lady Isabella, daughter of that prince, whom thou hast basely, and traitorously got into thy power, by bribing her false guardians during his absence; and he requires thee to resign the principality of Otranto, which thou hast usurped from the said Lord Frederic, the nearest of blood to the last rightful lord, Alfonso the good. If thou dost not instantly comply with these just demands, he defies thee to single combat to the last extremity." And so saying, the herald cast down his warder.

"And where is this braggart, who sends thee?" said Manfred. "At the distance of a league," said the herald: "he comes to make good his lord's claim against thee, as he is a true knight, and thou an usurper and ravisher."

Injurious as this challenge was, Manfred reflected that it was not his interest to provoke the Marquis. He knew how well founded the claim of Frederic was; nor was this the first time he had heard of it. Frederic's ancestors had assumed the stile of princes of Otranto, from the death of Alfonso the good without issue: but Manfred, his father, and grandfather, had been too powerful for the house of Vicenza to dispossess them. Frederic, a martial and amorous young prince, had married a beautiful young lady of whom he was enamoured, and who had died in childbed of Isabella. Her death affected him so much, that he had taken the cross, and gone to the holy land, where he was wounded in an engagement against the infidels, made prisoner, and reported to be dead. When the news reached Manfred's ears, he bribed the guardians of the Lady Isabella to deliver her up to him, as a bride for his son Conrad, by which alliance he had proposed to unite the claims of the two houses. This motive, on Conrad's death, had co-operated to make him so suddenly resolve on espousing her himself; and the same reflection determined him now to endeavour at obtaining the consent of Frederic to this marriage. A like policy inspired him with the thought of inviting

Frederic's champion into his castle, lest he should be informed of Isabella's flight, which he strictly enjoined his domestics not to disclose to any of the knight's retinue.

"Herald," said Manfred, as soon as he had digested these reflections, "return to thy master, and tell him ere we liquidate our differences by the sword, Manfred would hold some converse with him. Bid him welcome to my castle, where, by my faith, as I am a true knight, he shall have courteous reception, and full security for himself and followers. If we cannot adjust our quarrel by amicable means, I swear he shall depart in safety, and shall have full satisfaction, according to the laws of arms: so help me God, and his holy Trinity!" The herald made three obeisances and retired.

During this interview, Jerome's mind was agitated by a thousand contrary passions. He trembled for the life of his son, and his first thought was to persuade Isabella to return to the castle. Yet he was scarce less alarmed at the thought of her union with Manfred. He dreaded Hippolita's unbounded submission to the will of her lord; and though he did not doubt but he could alarm her piety not to consent to a divorce, if he could get access to her; yet, should Manfred discover that the obstruction came from him, it might be equally fatal to Theodore. He was impatient to know whence came the herald, who, with so little management, had questioned the title of Manfred: yet he did not dare absent himself from the convent, lest Isabella should leave it, and her flight be imputed to him. He returned disconsolately to the monastery, uncertain on what conduct to resolve. A monk, who met him in the porch, and observed his melancholy air, said, "Alas! brother, is it then true that we have lost our excellent princess Hippolita?" The holy man started, and cried, "What meanest thou, brother? I come this instant from the castle, and left her in perfect health." "Martelli," replied the other friar, "passed by the convent, but a quarter of an hour ago, on his way from the castle, and reported that her highness was dead. All our brethren are gone to the chapel to pray for her happy transit to a better life, and willed me to wait thy arrival. They know thy holy attachment to that good lady, and are anxious for the affliction it will cause in thee; indeed we have all reason to weep; she was a mother to our house; but this life is but a pilgrimage; we must not murmur; we shall all follow her! may our end be like hers!" "Good brother, thou dreamest," said Jerome: "I tell thee I come from the castle, and left the princess well. Where is the Lady Isabella?" "Poor gentlewoman!" replied the friar; "I told her the sad news, and offered her spiritual comfort; I reminded her of the transitory condition of mortality, and advised her to take the veil: I quoted the example of the holy princess Sanchia of Arragon." "Thy zeal was laudable," said Jerome, impatiently; "but at present it was unnecessary: Hippolita is well; at least I trust in the Lord she is; I heard nothing to the contrary; yet, methinks, the prince's earnestness—well, brother, but where is the Lady Isabella?" "I know not," said the friar; "she wept much, and said she would retire to her chamber."

Jerome left his comrade abruptly, and hastened to the princess, but she was not in her chamber. He enquired of the domestics of the convent, but could learn no news of her. He searched in vain throughout the monastery and the church, and dispatched messengers round the neighbourhood, to get intelligence if she had been seen; but to no purpose. Nothing could equal the good man's perplexity. He judged that Isabella, suspecting Manfred of having precipitated his wife's death, had taken the alarm, and withdrawn herself to some more secret place of concealment. This new flight would probably carry the prince's fury to the height. The report of Hippolita's death, though it seemed almost incredible, increased his consternation; and though Isabella's escape bespoke her aversion of Manfred for a husband, Jerome could feel no comfort from it, while it endangered the life of his son. He determined to return to the castle, and made several of his brethren accompany him to attest his innocence to Manfred, and, if necessary, join their intercessions with his for Theodore.

The prince, in the mean time, had passed into the court, and ordered the gates of the castle to be flung open, for the reception of the stranger knight and his train. In a few minutes the cavalcade arrived. First came two harbingers with wands. Next a herald, followed by two pages and two trumpeters. Then an hundred foot guards. These were attended by as many horse. After them fifty footmen, cloathed in scarlet and black, the colours of the knight. Then a led horse. Two heralds on each side of a gentleman on horseback, bearing a banner, with the arms of Vicenza and Otranto quarterly; a circumstance that much offended Manfred, but he stifled his resentment. Two more pages. The knight's confessor, telling his beads. Fifty more footmen, clad as before. Two knights, habited in complete armour, their beavers down, comrades to the principal knight. The squires of the two knights, carrying their shields and devices. The knight's own squire. An hundred gentlemen, bearing an enormous sword, and seeming to faint under the weight of it. The knight himself on a chestnut steed, in complete armour, his lance in the rest, his face entirely concealed by his vizor, which was surmounted by a large plume of scarlet and black feathers. Fifty foot guards, with drums and trumpets, closed the procession, which wheeled off to the right and left, to make room for the principal knight.

As soon as he approached the gate, he stopped; and the herald advancing, read again the words of the challenge. Manfred's eyes were fixed on the gigantic sword, and he scarce seemed to attend to the cartel: but his attention was soon diverted by a tempest of wind that rose behind him. He turned and beheld the plumes of the enchanted helmet, agitated in the same extraordinary manner as before. It required intrepidity like Manfred's not to sink under a concurrence of circumstances, that seemed to announce his fate. Yet scorning, in the presence of strangers, to betray the courage he had always manifested, he said boldly, "Sir knight, whoever thou art, I bid thee welcome. If thou art of mortal mould, thy valour shall meet its equal: and if thou art a true knight, thou wilt scorn to employ sorcery to carry thy point. Be these omens from heaven or hell, Manfred trusts to the righteousness of his cause, and to the aid of St. Nicholas, who has ever protected his house. Alight, Sir knight, and repose thyself: to-morrow thou shalt have a fair field; and heaven befriend the juster side!"

The knight made no reply, but dismounting, was conducted by Manfred to the great hall of the castle. As they traversed the court, the knight stopped to gaze on the miraculous casque; and, kneeling down, seemed to pray inwardly for some minutes. Rising, he made a sign to the prince to lead on. As soon as they entered the hall, Manfred proposed to the stranger to disarm, but the knight shook his head in token of refusal. "Sir knight," said Manfred, "this is not courteous; but, by my good faith, I will not cross thee; nor shalt thou have cause to complain of the prince of Otranto. No treachery is designed on my part; I hope none is intended on thine; here, take my gage (giving him his ring); your friends and you shall enjoy the laws of hospitality. Rest here, until refreshments are brought: I will but give orders for the accommodation of your train, and return to you." The three knights bowed, as accepting his courtesy. Manfred directed the stranger's retinue to be conducted to an adjacent hospital, founded by the princess Hippolita for the reception of pilgrims. As they made the circuit of the court to return towards the gate, the gigantic sword burst from the supporters, and, falling to the ground opposite to the helmet, remained immoveable. Manfred, almost hardened to preternatural appearances, surmounted the shock of his new prodigy; and returning to the hall, where by this time the feast was ready, he invited his silent guests to take their places. Manfred, however ill his heart was at ease, endeavoured to inspire the company with mirth. He put several questions to them, but was answered only by signs. They raised their vizors but sufficiently to feed themselves, and that but sparingly. "Sirs," said the prince, "ye are the first guests I ever treated within these walls, who scorned to hold intercourse with me; nor has it oft been customary, I ween, for princes to hazard their state and dignity against strangers and mutes. You say you come in the name of Frederic of Vicenza; I have heard that he was a gallant and courteous knight; nor would he, I am bold to say, think it beneath him to mix in social converse with a prince who is his equal, and not unknown by deeds in arms. Still ye are silent—well! be it as it may; by the laws of hospitality and chivalry, ye are masters under this roof; ye shall do your pleasure—but come, give me a goblet of wine; ye will not refuse to pledge me to the healths of your fair mistresses?" The principal knight sighed and crossed himself, and was rising from the board—"Sir knight," said Manfred, "what I said was but in sport: I shall constrain you in nothing; use your good liking. Since mirth is not your mood, let us be sad. Business may hit your fancies better: let us withdraw; and hear if what I have to unfold, may be better relished, than the vain efforts I have made for your pastime."

Manfred, then conducting the three knights into an inner chamber, shut the door, and inviting them to be seated, began thus, addressing himself to the chief personage.

"You come, Sir knight, as I understand, in the name of the Marquis of Vicenza, to re-demand the Lady Isabella, his daughter, who has been contracted, in the face of holy church, to my son, by the consent of her legal guardians; and to require me to resign my dominions to your lord, who gives himself for the nearest of blood to prince Alfonso, whose soul God rest! I shall speak to the latter article of your demands first. You must know—your lord knows, that I enjoy the principality of Otranto from my father Don Manuel, as he received it from his father Don Ricardo. Alfonso, their predecessor, dying childless in the Holy Land, bequeathed his estates to my grandfather Don Ricardo, in consideration of his faithful services." The stranger shook his head—"Sir knight," said Manfred, warmly, "Ricardo was a valiant and upright man; he was a pious man; witness his munificent foundation of the adjoining church and two convents. He was peculiarly patronised by St. Nicholas—my grandfather was incapable—I say, sir, Don Ricardo was incapable—excuse me, your interruption has disordered me. I venerate the memory of my grandfather—well! Sirs, he held this estate; he held it by his good sword, and by the favour of St. Nicholas—so did my father; and so, sirs, will I, come what come will—but Frederic, your lord, is nearest in blood —I have consented to put my title to the issue of the sword—does that imply a vicious title? I might have asked, where is Frederic your lord? Report speaks him dead in captivity. You say, your actions say, he lives—I question it not—I might, sirs, I might, but I do not. Other princes would bid Frederic take his inheritance by force, if he can; they would not stake their dignity on a single combat—they would not submit it to the decision of unknown mutes—pardon me, gentlemen, I am too warm; but suppose yourselves in my situation; as ye are stout knights, would it not move your choler, to have your own, and the honour of your ancestors, called in question? but to the point. Ye require me to deliver up the Lady Isabella—Sirs, I must ask if ye are authorised to receive her?" The knight nodded. "Receive her," continued Manfred; "well! you are authorised to receive her; but, gentle knight, may I ask if you have full powers?" The knight nodded. "'Tis well," said Manfred; "then hear what I have to offer: ye see, gentlemen, before you, the most unhappy of men! (he began to weep) afford me your compassion; I am entitled to it; indeed I am. Know, I have lost my only hope, my joy, the support of my house—Conrad died yester-morning." The knights discovered signs of surprise. "Yes, sirs, fate has disposed of my son; Isabella is at liberty"—"Do you then restore her?" cried the chief knight, breaking silence. "Afford me your patience," said Manfred. "I rejoice to find, by this testimony of your good will, that this matter may be adjusted without blood. It is no interest of mine dictates what little I have farther to say. Ye behold in me a man disgusted with the world: the loss of my son has weaned me from earthly cares. Power and greatness have no longer any charms in my eyes. I wished to transmit the sceptre I had received from my ancestors with honour to my son—but that is over! life itself is so indifferent to me, that I accepted your defiance with joy: a good knight cannot go to the grave with more satisfaction, than when falling in his vocation: whatever is the will of heaven, I submit; for, alas! sirs, I am a man of many sorrows. Manfred is no object of envy—but no doubt you are acquainted with my story." The knight made signs of ignorance, and seemed curious to have Manfred proceed. "Is it possible, sirs," continued the prince, "that my story should be a secret to you; have you heard nothing relating to me and the princess Hippolita?" They shook their heads. "No! thus then, sirs, it is. You think me ambitious: ambition, alas! is composed of more rugged materials. If I were ambitious, I should not, for so many years, have been prey to all the hell of conscientious scruples—but I weary your patience: I will be brief. Know then, that I have long been troubled in mind on my union with the princess Hippolita. Oh! sirs, if ye were acquainted with that excellent woman! if ye knew that I adore her like a mistress, and cherish her as a friend—but man was not born for perfect happiness! she shares my scruples, and, with her consent, I have brought this matter before the church, for we are related within the forbidden degrees. I expect every hour the definitive sentence that must separate us for ever—I am sure you feel for me—I see you do—pardon these tears!" The knights gazed on each other, wondering where this would end. Manfred continued: "The death of my son betiding, while my soul was under this anxiety, I thought of nothing but resigning my dominions, and retiring for ever from the sight of mankind. My only difficulty was to fix on a successor, who would be tender of my people, and to dispose of the Lady Isabella, who is dear to me as my own blood. I was willing to restore the line of Alfonso, even in his most distant kindred: and though, pardon me, I am satisfied it was his will, that Ricardo's lineage should take place of his own relations; yet where was I to search for those relations? I knew of none but Frederic your lord; he was a captive to the infidels, or dead; and were he living, and at home, would he quit the flourishing state of Vicenza, for the inconsiderable principality of Otranto? if he would not, could I bear the thought of seeing a hard, unfeeling viceroy set over my poor faithful people? for, sirs, I love my people, and, thank heaven, am beloved by them: but ye will ask, whither tends this long discourse? briefly then, thus, sirs. Heaven, in your arrival, seems to point out a remedy for those difficulties and my misfortunes. The Lady Isabella is at liberty; I shall soon be so. I would submit to anything for the good of my people—were it not the best, the only way to extinguish the feuds between our families, if I was to take the Lady Isabella to wife—you start—but, though Hippolita's virtues will ever be dear to me, a prince must not consider himself; he is born for his people." A servant at that instant entering the chamber, apprised Manfred that Jerome and several of his brethren demanded immediate access to him.

The prince, provoked at this interruption, and fearing that the friar would discover to the strangers that Isabella had taken sanctuary, was going to forbid Jerome's entrance. But recollecting that he was certainly arrived to notify the princess's return, Manfred began to excuse himself to the knights for leaving them for a few moments, but was prevented by the arrival of the friars. Manfred angrily reprimanded them for their intrusion, and would have forced them back from the chamber; but Jerome was too much agitated to be repulsed. He declared aloud the flight of Isabella, with protestations of his own innocence. Manfred, distracted at the news, and not less at its coming to the knowledge of the strangers, uttered nothing but incoherent sentences; now upbraiding the friar, now apologising to the knights, earnest to know what was become of Isabella, yet equally afraid of their knowing; impatient to pursue her, yet dreading to have them join in the pursuit. He offered to dispatch messengers in quest of her, but the chief knight, no longer keeping silence, reproached Manfred, in bitter terms, for his dark and ambiguous dealing, and demanded the cause of Isabella's first absence from the castle. Manfred, casting a stern look at Jerome, implying a command of silence, pretended that, on Conrad's death, he had placed her in sanctuary, until he could determine how to dispose of her. Jerome, who trembled for his son's life, did not dare to contradict this falsehood, but one of his brethren, not under the same anxi-

ety, declared, frankly, that she had fled to their church in the preceding night. The prince, in vain, endeavoured to stop this discovery, which overwhelmed him with shame and confusion. The
principal stranger, amazed at the contradictions he heard, and
more than half persuaded that Manfred had secreted the princess, notwithstanding the concern he expressed at her flight, rushing to the door, said, "Thou traitor prince! Isabella shall be
found." Manfred endeavoured to hold him, but the other knights
assisting their comrade, he broke from the prince, and hastened
into the court, demanding his attendants. Manfred, finding it in
vain to divert him from the pursuit, offered to accompany him,
and summoning his attendants, and taking Jerome and some of
the friars to guide them, they issued from the castle; Manfred
privately giving orders to have the knight's company secured,
while to the knight he affected to dispatch a messenger to require
their assistance.

The company had no sooner quitted the castle, than Matilda,
who felt herself deeply interested for the young peasant, since she
had seen him condemned to death in the hall, and whose thoughts
had been taken up with concerting measures to save him, was informed by some of the female attendants, that Manfred had dispatched all his men various ways in pursuit of Isabella. He had,
in his hurry, given this order in general terms, not meaning to ex-
tend it to the guard he had set upon Theodore, but forgetting it.
The domestics, officious to obey so peremptory a prince, and urged
by their own curiosity, and love of novelty, to join in any precipi-
tate chase, had, to a man, left the castle. Matilda disengaged
herself from her women, stole up to the black tower, and unbolt-
ing the door, presented herself to the astonished Theodore.
"Young man," said she, "though filial duty and womanly modesty
condemn the step I am taking, yet holy charity, surmounting all
other ties, justifies this act. Fly, the doors of thy prison are open:
my father and his domestics are absent, but they may soon return;
be gone in safety, and may the angels of heaven direct thy
course!"—"Thou art surely one of those angels!" said the en-
raptured Theodore: "none but a blessed saint could speak, could
act, could look, like thee!—May I not know the name of my divine protectress? Methought thou namedst thy father: is it possible? can Manfred's blood feel holy pity?—Lovely lady, thou
answerest not—but how art thou here thyself? why dost thou neg-

lect thy own safety, and waste a thought on a wretch like Theodore? Let us fly together: the life thou bestowest shall be dedicated to thy defence."—"Alas! thou mistakest," said Matilda, sighing; "I am Manfred's daughter, but no dangers await me."—"Amazement!" said Theodore; "but last night I blessed myself for yielding thee the service thy gracious compassion so charitably returns me now."—"Still thou art in an error," said the princess; "but this is no time for explanation. Fly, virtuous youth, while it is in my power to save thee: should my father return, thou and I both should, indeed, have cause to tremble."—"How," said Theodore, "thinkest thou, charming maid, that I will accept of life at the hazard of aught calamitous to thee? better I endured a thousand deaths."—"I run no risk," said Matilda, "but by thy delay. Depart, it cannot be known that I assisted thy flight."—"Swear by the saints above," said Theodore, "that thou canst not be suspected; else here I vow to await whatever can befal me"—"Oh! thou art too generous," said Matilda, "but rest assured that no suspicion can alight on me."—"Give me thy beauteous hand, in token that thou dost not deceive me," said Theodore, "and let me bathe it with the warm tears of gratitude."—"Forbear," said the princess, "this must not be."—"Alas!" said Theodore, "I have never known but calamity until this hour—perhaps shall never know other fortune again: suffer the chaste raptures of holy gratitude: 'tis my soul would print its effusions on thy hand."—"Forbear and be gone," said Matilda: "how would Isabella approve of seeing thee at my feet?"—"Who is Isabella?" said the young man, with surprise.—"Ah me! I fear," said the princess, "I am serving a deceitful one!—hast thou forgot thy curiosity this morning?"—"Thy looks, thy actions, all thy beauteous self, seems an emanation of divinity," said Theodore, "but thy words are dark and mysterious,—speak, lady; speak to thy servant's comprehension."—"Thou understandest but too well!" said Matilda: "but once more I command thee to be gone: thy blood, which I may preserve, will be on my head, if I waste the time in vain discourse."—"I go, lady," said Theodore, "because it is thy will, and because I would not bring the grey hairs of my father with sorrow to the grave. Say but, adored lady, that I have thy gentle pity."—"Stay," said Matilda, "I will conduct thee to the subterraneous vault by which Isabella escaped; it will lead thee to the church of St. Nicholas, where thou mayest take sanctuary."—"What," said

Theodore, "was it another, and not thy lovely self, that I assisted to find the subterraneous passage?"—"It was," said Matilda, "but ask no more: I tremble to see thee still abide here: fly to the sanctuary."—"To sanctuary," said Theodore, "no, princess, sanctuaries are for helpless damsels, or for criminals. Theodore's soul is free from guilt, nor will wear the appearance of it. Give me a sword, lady, and thy father shall learn that Theodore scorns an ignominious flight."—"Rash youth!" said Matilda, "thou wouldst not dare to lift thy presumptuous arm against the Prince of Otranto?"—"Not against thy father, indeed, I dare not;" said Theodore, "excuse me, lady, I had forgotten—but could I gaze on thee, and remember thou art sprung from the tyrant Manfred? —but he is thy father, and, from this moment, my injuries are buried in oblivion." A deep and hollow groan, which seemed to come from above, startled the princess and Theodore. "Good heaven! we are overheard!" said the princess. They listened, but perceiving no further noise, they both concluded it the effect of pent-up vapours; and the princess, preceding Theodore softly, carried him to her father's armoury, where, equipping him with a complete suit, he was conducted by Matilda to the postern gate. "Avoid the town," said the princess, "and all the western side of the castle: 'tis there the search must be making by Manfred and the strangers: but hie thee to the opposite quarter. Yonder, behind that forest, to the east, is a chain of rocks, hollowed into a labyrinth of caverns, that reach to the sea-coast. There thou mayest lie concealed, till thou canst make signs to some vessel to put on shore and take thee off. Go; heaven be thy guide!—and sometimes in thy prayers remember—Matilda!" Theodore flung himself at her feet, and seizing her lily hand, which with struggles she suffered him to kiss, he vowed, on the earliest opportunity, to get himself knighted, and fervently entreated her permission to swear himself eternally her knight.—Ere the princess could reply, a clap of thunder was suddenly heard, that shook the battlements. Theodore, regardless of the tempest, would have urged his suit; but the princess, dismayed, retreated hastily into the castle, and commanded the youth to be gone, with an air that would not be disobeyed. He sighed, and retired, but with eyes fixed on the gate, until Matilda, closing it, put an end to an interview, in which the hearts of both had drunk so deeply of a passion, which both now tasted for the first time.

Theodore went pensively to the convent, to acquaint his father with his deliverance. There he learned the absence of Jerome, and the pursuit that was making after the Lady Isabella, with some particulars of whose story he now first became acquainted. The generous gallantry of his nature prompted him to wish to assist her; but the monks could lend him no lights to guess at the route she had taken. He was not tempted to wander far in search of her, for the idea of Matilda had imprinted itself so strongly on his heart, that he could not bear to absent himself at much distance from her abode. The tenderness Jerome had expressed for him concurred to confirm this reluctance; and he even persuaded himself that filial affection was the chief cause of his hovering between the castle and monastery. Until Jerome should return at night, Theodore at length determined to repair to the forest that Matilda had pointed out to him. Arriving there, he sought the gloomiest shades, as best suited to the pleasing melancholy that reigned in his mind. In this mood he roved insensibly to the caves which had formerly served as a retreat to hermits, and were now reported round the country to be haunted by evil spirits. He recollected to have heard this tradition; and being of a brave and adventurous disposition, he willingly indulged his curiosity in exploring the secret recesses of this labyrinth. He had not penetrated far, before he thought he heard the steps of some person who seemed to retreat before him. Theodore, though firmly grounded in all our holy faith enjoins to be believed, had no apprehension that good men were abandoned, without cause, to the malice of the powers of darkness. He thought the place more likely to be infested by robbers than by those infernal agents who are reported to molest and bewilder travellers. He had long burned with impatience to approve his valour—drawing his sabre, he marched sedately onwards, still directing his steps, as the imperfect rustling sound before him led the way. The armour he wore was a like indication to the person who avoided him. Theodore, now convinced that he was not mistaken, redoubled his pace, and evidently gained on the person that fled, whose haste increasing, Theodore came up just as a woman fell breathless before him. He hastened to raise her, but her terror was so great, that he apprehended she would faint in his arms. He used every gentle word to dispel her alarms, and assured her, that, far from injuring, he would defend her at the peril of his life. The lady, recovering her spirits from his courteous demeanour, and gazing on her protector, said, "Sure I have heard that voice before!"—"Not to my knowledge," replied Theodore, "unless, as I conjecture, thou art the Lady Isabella."—"Merciful heaven!" cried she, "thou art not sent in quest of me, art thou?" and saying those words, she threw herself at his feet, and besought him not to deliver her up to Manfred. "To Manfred!" cried Theodore —"no, lady; I have once already delivered thee from his tyranny, and it shall fare hard with me now, but I place thee out of the reach of his daring."—"Is it possible," said she, "that thou shouldst be the generous unknown whom I met last night in the vault of the castle? Sure thou art not a mortal, but my guardian angel. On my knees let me thank"—"Hold, gentle princess," said Theodore, "nor demean thyself before a poor and friendless young man. If heaven has selected me for thy deliverer, it will accomplish its work, and strengthen my arm in thy cause—but come, lady, we are too near the mouth of the cavern; let us seek its inmost recesses: I can have no tranquillity till I have placed thee beyond the reach of danger."—"Alas! what mean you, sir?" said she. "Though all your actions are noble, though your sentiments speak the purity of your soul, is it fitting that I should accompany you alone into these perplexed retreats? should we be found together, what would a censorious world think of my conduct?"— "I respect your virtuous delicacy," said Theodore; "nor do you harbour a suspicion that wounds my honour. I meant to conduct you into the most private cavity of these rocks, and then, at the hazard of my life, to guard their entrance against every living thing. Besides, lady," continued he, drawing a deep sigh, "beauteous and all-perfect as your form is, and though my wishes are not guiltless of aspiring, know, my soul is dedicated to another; and although"——a sudden noise prevented Theodore from proceeding. They soon distinguished these sounds, "Isabella! what ho! Isabella!"—the trembling princess relapsed into her former agony of fear. Theodore endeavoured to encourage her, but in vain. He assured her he would die rather than suffer her to return under Manfred's power; and, begging her to remain concealed, he went forth to prevent the person in search of her from approaching.

At the mouth of the cavern he found an armed knight, discoursing with a peasant, who assured him he had seen a lady enter the passes of the rock. The knight was preparing to seek her, when Theodore, placing himself in his way, with his sword drawn, sternly forbade him, at his peril, to advance. "And who art thou, who darest to cross my way?" said the knight, haughtily. "One who does not dare more than he will perform," said Theodore. "I seek the Lady Isabella," said the knight, "and understand she has taken refuge among these rocks. Impede me not, or thou wilt repent having provoked my resentment." "Thy purpose is as odious as thy resentment is contemptible," said Theodore. "Return whence thou camest, or we shall soon know whose resentment is most terrible." The stranger, who was the principal knight that had arrived from the Marquis of Vicenza, had galloped from Manfred as he was busied in getting information of the princess, and giving various orders to prevent her falling into the power of the three knights. Their chief had suspected Manfred of being privy to the princess's absconding; and this insult from a man, who, he concluded, was stationed by that prince to secrete her, confirming his suspicions, he made no reply, but discharging a blow with his sabre at Theodore, would soon have removed all obstruction, if Theodore, who took him for one of Manfred's captains, and who had no sooner given the provocation than prepared to support it, had not received the stroke on his shield. The valour that had so long been smothered in his breast, broke forth at once; he rushed impetuously on the knight, whose pride and wrath were not less powerful incentives to hardy deeds. The combat was furious, but not long: Theodore wounded the knight in three several places, and at last disarmed him, as he fainted by the loss of blood. The peasant, who had fled on the first onset, had given the alarm to some of Manfred's domestics, who, by his orders, were dispersed through the forest, in pursuit of Isabella. They came up as the knight fell, whom they soon discovered to be the noble stranger. Theodore, notwithstanding his hatred to Manfred, could not behold the victory he had gained, without emotions of pity and generosity: but he was more touched when he learned the quality of his adversary, and was informed that he was no retainer, but an enemy of Manfred. He assisted the servants of the latter in disarming the knight, and in endeavouring to staunch the blood that flowed from his wounds. The knight, recovering his speech, said, in a faint and faltering voice, "Generous foe, we have both been in an error: I took thee for an instrument of the tyrant; I perceive thou hast made the like mistake—

it is too late for excuses—I faint—if Isabella is at hand—call her —I have important secrets to"—"He is dying!" said one of the attendants; "has nobody a crucifix about them? Andrea, do thou pray over him."—"Fetch some water," said Theodore, "and pour it down his throat, while I hasten to the princess."—Saying this, he flew to Isabella, and, in few words, told her, modestly, that he had been so unfortunate, by mistake, as to wound a gentleman from her father's court, who wished, ere he died, to impart something of consequence to her.—The princess, who had been transported at hearing the voice of Theodore, as he called her to come forth, was astonished at what she heard. Suffering herself to be conducted by Theodore, the new proof of whose valour recalled her dispersed spirits, she came where the bleeding knight lay speechless on the ground—but her fears returned, when she beheld the domestics of Manfred. She would again have fled, if Theodore had not made her observe that they were unarmed, and had not threatened them with instant death, if they should dare to seize the princess. The stranger opening his eyes, and beholding a woman, said,—"Art thou—pray, tell me truly—art thou Isabella of Vicenza?"—"I am," said she; "Good heaven restore thee!" —"Then thou—then thou"—said the knight, struggling for utterance—"seest—thy father—give me one"—"Oh! amazement! horror! what do I hear! what do I see!" cried Isabella. "My father! you my father! how came you here, sir? for heaven's sake speak!— oh! run for help, or he will expire!"—"'Tis most true," said the wounded knight, exerting all his force; "I am Frederic, thy father —yes, I came to deliver thee—It will not be—give me a parting kiss, and take"—"Sir," said Theodore, "do not exhaust yourself: suffer us to convey you to the castle."—"To the castle!" said Isabella; "is there no help nearer than the castle? would you expose my father to the tyrant? if he goes thither, I dare not accompany him—and yet can I leave him!" "My child," said Frederic, "it matters not for me whither I am carried: a few minutes will place me beyond danger—but while I have eyes to doat on thee, forsake me not, dear Isabella! This brave knight—I know not who he is, will protect thy innocence—Sir, you will not abandon my child, will you?"—Theodore, shedding tears over his victim, and vowing to guard the princess at the expense of his life, persuaded Frederic to suffer himself to be conducted to the castle. They placed him on a horse belonging to one of the domestics, after

binding up his wounds as well as they were able. Theodore
marched by his side, and the afflicted Isabella, who could not bear
to quit him, followed mournfully behind.

CHAPTER IV

The sorrowful troop no sooner arrived at the castle, than they
were met by Hippolita and Matilda, whom Isabella had sent one
of the domestics before to advertise of their approach. The ladies,
causing Frederic to be conveyed into the nearest chamber, retired, while the surgeons examined his wounds. Matilda blushed
at seeing Theodore and Isabella together; but endeavoured to
conceal it by embracing the latter, and condoling with her on her
father's mischance. The surgeons soon came to acquaint Hippolita that none of the marquis's wounds were dangerous; and that
he was desirous of seeing his daughter and the princesses. Theodore, under pretence of expressing his joy at being freed from his
apprehensions of the combat being fatal to Frederic, could not
resist the impulse of following Matilda. Her eyes were so often
cast down, on meeting his, that Isabella, who regarded Theodore
as attentively as he gazed on Matilda, soon divined who the object
was that he had told her, in the cave, engaged his affections. While
this mute scene passed, Hippolita demanded of Frederic the
cause of his having taken that mysterious course for reclaiming
his daughter; and threw in various apologies to excuse her lord
for the match contracted between their children. Frederic, however incensed against Manfred, was not insensible to the courtesy
and benevolence of Hippolita: but he was still more struck with
the lovely form of Matilda. Wishing to detain them by his bed-
side, he informed Hippolita of his story. He told her, that, while
prisoner to the infidels, he had dreamed that his daughter, of
whom he had learned no news since his captivity, was detained in
a castle, where she was in danger of the most dreadful misfortunes: and that if he obtained his liberty, and repaired to a wood
near Joppa, he would learn more. Alarmed at this dream, and incapable of obeying the direction given by it, his chains became
more grievous than ever. But while his thoughts were occupied
on the means of obtaining his liberty, he received the agreeable

news, that the confederate princes, who were warring in Palestine, had paid his ransom. He instantly set out for the wood that had been marked in his dream. For three days he and his attendants had wandered in the forest, without seeing a human form; but, on the evening of the third, they came to a cell, in which they found a venerable hermit in the agonies of death. Applying rich cordials, they brought the saint-like man to his speech. "My sons," said he, "I am bounden to your charity—but it is in vain—I am going to my eternal rest—yet I die with the satisfaction of performing the will of heaven. When first I repaired to this solitude, after seeing my country become a prey to unbelievers—it is, alas! above fifty years since I was witness to that dreadful scene!—St. Nicholas appeared to me, and revealed a secret, which he bade me never disclose to mortal man, but on my death-bed. This is that tremendous hour, and ye are, no doubt, the chosen warriors to whom I was ordered to reveal my trust. As soon as ye have done the last offices to this wretched corse, dig under the seventh tree on the left hand of this poor cave, and your pains will—Oh! good heaven receive my soul!" With those words, the devout man breathed his last. "By break of day," continued Frederic, "when we had committed the holy relics to earth, we dug according to direction—but what was our astonishment, when, about the depth of six feet, we discovered an enormous sabre—the very weapon yonder in the court. On the blade, which was then partly out of the scabbard, though since closed by our efforts in removing it, were written the following lines—no; excuse me, madam," added the marquis, turning to Hippolita, "if I forbear to repeat them: I respect your sex and rank, and would not be guilty of offending your ear with sounds injurious to aught that is dear to you." —He paused: Hippolita trembled. She did not doubt but Frederic was destined by heaven to accomplish the fate that seemed to threaten her house. Looking with anxious fondness at Matilda, a silent tear stole down her cheek; but recollecting herself, she said, "Proceed, my lord; heaven does nothing in vain; mortals must receive its divine behests with lowliness and submission. It is our part to deprecate its wrath, or bow to its decrees. Repeat the sentence, my lord, we listen resigned." Frederic was grieved that he had proceeded so far. The dignity and patient firmness of Hippolita penetrated him with respect, and the tender silent affection with which the princess and her daughter regarded each other,

melted him almost to tears. Yet, apprehensive that his forbear-
ance to obey would be more alarming, he repeated, in a faltering
and low voice, the following lines:—

> "Where'er a casque that suits this sword is found,
> With perils is thy daughter compass'd round;
> Alfonso's blood alone can save the maid,
> And quiet a long restless prince's shade."

"What is there in these lines," said Theodore impatiently, "that
affects these princesses? why were they to be shocked by a mysterious delicacy, that has so little foundation?"—"Your words are
rude, young man," said the marquis; "and though fortune has
favoured you once"—"My honoured lord," said Isabella, who
resented Theodore's warmth, which she perceived was dictated
by his sentiments for Matilda, "discompose not yourself for the
glosing of a peasant's son: he forgets the reverence he owes you;
but he is not accustomed"—Hippolita, concerned at the heat that
had arisen, checked Theodore for his boldness, but with an air
acknowledging his zeal; and, changing the conversation, demanded of Frederic where he had left her lord? As the marquis
was going to reply, they heard a noise without, and rising to inquire the cause, Manfred, Jerome, and part of the troop, who had
met an imperfect rumour of what had happened, entered the
chamber. Manfred advanced hastily towards Frederic's bed, to
condole with him on his misfortune, and to learn the circumstances of the combat, when, starting in an agony of terror and
amazement, he cried, "Ha! what art thou? thou dreadful spectre!
is my hour come?"—"My dearest, gracious lord," cried Hippolita,
clasping him in her arms, "what is it you see? why do you fix
your eye-balls thus?"—"What!" cried Manfred, breathless, "dost
thou see nothing, Hippolita? is this ghastly phantom sent to me
alone—to me, who did not"—"For mercy's sweetest self, my
lord," said Hippolita, "resume your soul, command your reason.
There is none here but we, your friends."—"What! is not that
Alfonso?" cried Manfred: "Dost thou not see him? can it be my
brain's delirium?"—"This! my lord," said Hippolita; "this is
Theodore, the youth who has been so unfortunate"—"Theodore!"
said Manfred, mournfully, and striking his forehead—"Theodore,
or a phantom, he has unhinged the soul of Manfred—but how
comes he here? and how comes he in armour?"—"I believe
he went in search of Isabella," said Hippolita. "Of Isabella!"

said Manfred, relapsing into rage—"yes, yes, that is not doubt-ful—but how did he escape from durance in which I left him? was it Isabella, or this hypocritical old friar, that pro-cured his enlargement?"—"And would a parent be criminal, my lord," said Theodore, "if he meditated the deliverance of his child?" Jerome, amazed to hear himself, in a manner, accused by his son, and without foundation, knew not what to think. He could not comprehend how Theodore had escaped; how he came to be armed, and to encounter Frederic. Still he would not venture to ask any questions that might tend to inflame Manfred's wrath against his son. Jerome's silence convinced Manfred that he had contrived Theodore's release—"And is it thus, thou ungrateful old man," said the prince, addressing himself to the friar, "that thou repayest mine and Hippolita's bounties? And, not content with traversing my heart's nearest wishes, thou armest thy bastard, and bringest him into my own castle to insult me!"—"My lord," said Theodore, "you wrong my father: nor he nor I are capable of harbouring a thought against your peace. Is it insolence thus to surrender myself to your highness's pleasure?" added he, lay-ing his sword respectfully at Manfred's feet. "Behold my bosom; strike, my lord, if you suspect that a disloyal thought is lodged there. There is not a sentiment engraven on my heart, that does not venerate you and yours." The grace and fervour with which Theodore uttered these words, interested every person present in his favour.—Even Manfred was touched—yet still possessed with his resemblance to Alfonso, his admiration was dashed with secret horror. "Rise," said he; "thy life is not my present purpose. But tell me thy history, and how thou camest connected with this old traitor here."—"My lord," said Jerome, eagerly—"Peace, im-postor," said Manfred; "I will not have him prompted."—"My lord," said Theodore, "I want no assistance. My story is very brief. I was carried, at five years of age, to Algiers, with my mother, who had been taken by corsairs from the coast of Sicily. She died of grief in less than a twelvemonth." The tears gushed from Jerome's eyes, on whose countenance a thousand anxious passions stood expressed. "Before she died," continued Theodore, "she bound a writing about my arm under my garments, which told me I was the son of the Count Falconara."—"It is most true," said Jerome; "I am that wretched father."—"Again I enjoin thee silence," said Manfred; "proceed."—"I remained in slavery," said Theodore, "until within these two years, when attending on my master in his cruises, I was delivered by a Christian vessel, which overpowered the pirate; and discovering myself to the captain, he generously put me on shore in Sicily—but alas! instead of finding a father, I learned that his estate, which was situated on the coast, had, during his absence, been laid waste by the Rover, who had carried my mother and me into captivity; that his castle had been burnt to the ground, and that my father, on his return, had sold what remained, and was retired into religion in the kingdom of Naples, but where no man could inform me. Destitute and friendless, hopeless almost of attaining the transport of a parent's embrace, I took the first opportunity of setting sail for Naples, from whence, within these six days, I wandered into this province, still supporting myself by the labour of my hands; nor until yestermorn did I believe that heaven had reserved any lot for me but peace of mind and contented poverty. This, my lord, is Theodore's story. I am blessed, beyond my hope, in finding a father: I am unfortunate, beyond my desert, in having incurred your highness's displeasure." He ceased. A murmur of approbation gently arose from the audience. "This is not all," said Frederic: "I am bound in honour to add what he suppresses. Though he is modest, I must be generous—he is one of the bravest youths on Christian ground. He is warm too; and, from the short knowledge I have of him, I will pledge myself for his veracity: if what he reports of himself were not true, he would not utter it—and for me, youth, I honour a frankness which becomes thy birth. But now, and thou didst offend me: yet the noble blood, which flows in thy veins, may well be allowed to boil out, when it has so recently traced itself to its source. Come, my lord," turning to Manfred, "if I can pardon him, surely you may. It is not the youth's fault, if you took him for a spectre." This bitter taunt galled the soul of Manfred. "If beings from another world," replied he, haughtily, "have power to impress my mind with awe, it is more than living man can do; nor could a stripling's arm"—"My lord," interrupted Hippolita, "your guest has occasion for repose: shall we not leave him to rest?" Saying this, and taking Manfred by the hand, she took leave of Frederic, and led the company forth. The prince, not sorry to quit a conversation, which recalled to mind the discovery he had made of his most secret sensations, suffered himself to be conducted to his own apartment, after permitting

Theodore, though under engagement to return to the castle on the morrow—a condition the young man gladly accepted—to retire with his father to the convent. Matilda and Isabella were too much occupied with their own reflections, and too little content with each other, to wish for farther converse that night. They separated each to her chamber, with more expressions of ceremony, and fewer of affection, than had passed between them since their childhood.

If they parted with small cordiality, they did but meet with greater impatience as soon as the sun was risen. Their minds were in a situation that excluded sleep, and each recollected a thousand questions which she wished she had put to the other overnight. Matilda reflected that Isabella had been twice delivered by Theodore in very critical situations, which she could not believe accidental. His eyes, it was true, had been fixed on her in Frederic's chamber; but that might have been to disguise his passion for Isabella from the fathers of both. It were better to clear this up. She wished to know the truth, lest she should wrong her friend, by entertaining a passion for Isabella's lover. Thus jealousy prompted, and, at the same time, borrowed an excuse from friendship to justify its curiosity.

Isabella, not less restless, had better foundation for her suspicions. Both Theodore's tongue and eyes had told her his heart was engaged—it was true—yet, perhaps, Matilda might not correspond to his passion—she had ever appeared insensible to love: all her thoughts were set on heaven.—"Why did I dissuade her?" said Isabella to herself: "I am punished for my generosity—but when did they meet? where? It cannot be: I have deceived myself—perhaps last night was the first time they ever beheld each other; it must be some other object that has prepossessed his affections; if it is, I am not so unhappy as I thought; if it is not my friend Matilda—how! can I stoop to wish for the affection of a man, who rudely and unnecessarily acquainted me with his indifference! and that, at the very moment in which common courtesy demanded at least expressions of civility. I will go to my dear Matilda, who will confirm me in this becoming pride—man is false—I will advise with her on taking the veil: she will rejoice to find me in this disposition; and I will acquaint her that I no longer oppose her inclination for the cloister." In this frame of mind, and determined to open her heart entirely to Matilda, she went to that princess's chamber, whom she found already dressed, and leaning pensively on her arm. This attitude, so correspondent to what she felt herself, revived Isabella's suspicions, and detroyed the confidence she had purposed to place in her friend. They blushed at meeting, and were too much novices to disguise their sensations with address. After some unmeaning questions and replies, Matilda demanded of Isabella the cause of her flight? The latter, who had almost forgotten Manfred's passion, so entirely was she occupied by her own, concluding that Matilda referred to her last escape from the convent, which had occasioned the events of the preceding evening, replied, "Martelli brought word to the convent that your mother was dead." "Oh!" said Matilda, interrupting her, "Bianca has explained that mistake to me: on seeing me faint, she cried out, 'The princess is dead!' and Martelli, who had come for the usual dole to the castle"—"And what made you faint?" said Isabella, indifferent to the rest.—Matilda blushed, and stammered—"My father—he was sitting in judgment on a criminal."—"What criminal?" said Isabella, eagerly. "A young man," said Matilda; "I believe—I think it was that young man that"—"What, Theodore?" said Isabella. "Yes!" answered she; "I never saw him before; I do not know how he had offended my father—but as he has been of service to you, I am glad my lord has pardoned him."—"Served me!" replied Isabella, "do you term it serving me, to wound my father, and almost occasion his death? Though it is but since yesterday that I am blessed with knowing a parent, I hope Matilda does not think I am such a stranger to filial tenderness as not to resent the boldness of that audacious youth, and that it is impossible for me ever to feel any affection for one who dared to lift his arm against the author of my being. No, Matilda, my heart abhors him; and if you still retain the friendship for me that you have vowed from your infancy, you will detest a man who has been on the point of making me miserable for ever." Matilda held down her head, and replied, "I hope my dearest Isabella does not doubt her Matilda's friendship: I never beheld that youth until yesterday; he is almost a stranger to me: but, as the surgeons have pronounced your father out of danger, you ought not to harbour uncharitable resentment against one, who, I am persuaded, did not know the marquis was related to you." "You plead his cause very pathetically," said Isabella, "considering he is so much a stranger to you! I am mistaken, or he returns your charity."—"What mean you?" said Matilda. "Nothing," said Isabella: repenting that she had given Matilda a hint of Theodore's inclination for her. Then, changing the discourse, she asked Matilda what occasioned Manfred to take Theodore for a spectre? "Bless me," said Matilda, "did not you observe his extreme resemblance to the portrait of Alfonso in the gallery? I took notice of it to Bianca even before I saw him in armour; but with the helmet on, he is the very image of that picture." "I do not much observe pictures," said Isabella; "much less have I examined this young man so attentively as you seem to have done —ah! Matilda, your heart is in danger—but let me warn you as a friend—he has owned to me that he is in love; it cannot be with you, for yesterday was the first time you ever met—was it not?" "Certainly," replied Matilda; "but why does my dearest Isabella conclude from anything I have said, that"—she paused—then continuing; "he saw you first, and I am far from having the vanity to think that my little portion of charms could engage a heart devoted to you—may you be happy, Isabella, whatever is the fate of Matilda!"—"My lovely friend," said Isabella, whose heart was too honest to resist a kind expression, "it is you that Theodore admires; I saw it; I am persuaded of it; nor shall a thought of my own happiness suffer me to interfere with yours." This frankness drew tears from the gentle Matilda; and jealousy, that, for a moment, had raised a coolness between these amiable maidens, soon gave way to the natural sincerity and candour of their souls. Each confessed to the other the impression that Theodore had made on her; and this confidence was followed by a struggle of generosity, each insisting on yielding her claim to her friend. At length, the dignity of Isabella's virtue reminding her of the preference which Theodore had almost declared for her rival, made her determine to conquer her passion, and cede the beloved object to her friend.

During this contest of amity, Hippolita entered her daughter's chamber. "Madam," said she to Isabella, "you have so much tenderness for Matilda, and interest yourself so kindly in whatever affects our wretched house, that I can have no secrets with my child which are not proper for you to hear." The princesses were all attention and anxiety. "Know then, madam," continued Hippolita, "and you, my dearest Matilda, that, being convinced, by all the events of these two last ominous days, that Heaven purposes the sceptre of Otranto should pass from Manfred's hands into those of the Marquis Frederic, I have been, perhaps, inspired with the thought of averting our total destruction by the union of our rival houses. With this view I have been proposing to Manfred, my lord, to tender this dear, dear child, to Frederic, your father"—"Me to Lord Frederic!" cried Matilda—"good heavens! my gracious mother—and have you named it to my father?"—"I have," said Hippolita; "he listened benignly to my proposal, and is gone to break it to the marquis."—"Ah! wretched princess!" cried Isabella; "what hast thou done! what ruin has thy inadvertent goodness been preparing for thyself, for me, and for Matilda!"—"Ruin from me to you and to my child!" said Hippolita, "what can this mean?"—"Alas!" said Isabella, "the purity of your own heart prevents your seeing the depravity of others. Manfred, your lord, that impious man"—"Hold," said Hippolita; "you must not, in my presence, young lady, mention Manfred with disrespect; he is my lord and husband, and"— "Will not long be so," said Isabella, "if his wicked purposes can be carried into execution."—"This language amazes me!" said Hippolita. "Your feeling, Isabella, is warm; but, until this hour, I never knew it betray you into intemperance. What deed of Manfred authorises you to treat him as a murderer, an assassin?" —"Thou virtuous, and too credulous princess!" replied Isabella; "it is not thy life he aims at—it is to separate himself from thee! to divorce thee! to"—"To divorce me!"—"To divorce my mother!" cried Hippolita and Matilda at once. "Yes," said Isabella; "and to complete his crime he meditates—I cannot speak it!"—"What can surpass what thou hast already uttered!" said Matilda. Hippolita was silent. Grief choked her speech; and the recollection of Manfred's late ambiguous discourses confirmed what she heard. "Excellent, dear lady! madam! mother!" cried Isabella, flinging herself at Hippolita's feet in a transport of passion; "trust me, believe me, I will die a thousand deaths sooner than consent to injure you, than yield to so odious—oh!"— "This is too much!" cried Hippolita: "What crimes does one crime suggest! Rise, dear Isabella; I do not doubt your virtue. Oh! Matilda, this stroke is too heavy for thee! weep not, my child! and not a murmur, I charge thee. Remember, he is thy father still!"—"But you are my mother too," said Matilda, fervently; "and you are virtuous, you are guiltless!—Oh! must not I, must not I complain?"—"You must not," said Hippolita; "come, all will yet be well. Manfred, in the agony for the loss of thy brother, knew not what he said: perhaps Isabella misunderstood him: his heart is good—and, my child, thou knowest not all! There is a destiny hangs over us; the hand of Providence is stretched out—Oh! could I but save thee from the wreck!—Yes," continued she, in a firmer tone; "perhaps the sacrifice of myself may atone for all—I will go and offer myself to this divorce—it boots not what becomes of me. I will withdraw into the neighbouring monastery, and waste the remainder of life in prayers and tears for my child and—the prince!"—"Thou art as much too good for this world," said Isabella, "as Manfred is execrable—but think not, lady, that thy weakness shall determine for me. I swear, hear me all ye angels"—"Stop, I adjure thee," cried Hippolita; "remember thou dost not depend on thyself; thou hast a father," —"My father is too pious, too noble," interrupted Isabella, "to command an impious deed. But should he command it; can a father enjoin a cursed act? I was contracted to the son, can I wed the father?—No, madam, no; force should not drag me to Manfred's hated bed. I loathe him, I abhor him: divine and human laws forbid—and my friend, my dearest Matilda! would I wound her tender soul by injuring her adored mother? my own mother— I never have known another."—"Oh! she is the mother of both!" cried Matilda: "Can we, can we, Isabella, adore her too much?"— "My lovely children," said the touched Hippolita, "your tenderness overpowers me—but I must not give way to it. It is not ours to make election for ourselves: heaven, our fathers, and our husbands, must decide for us. Have patience until you hear what Manfred and Frederic have determined. If the marquis accepts Matilda's hand, I know she will readily obey. Heaven may interpose and prevent the rest.—What means my child?" continued she, seeing Matilda fall at her feet with a flood of speechless tears —"But no; answer me not, my daughter: I must not hear a word against the pleasure of thy father."—"Oh! doubt not my obedience, my dreadful obedience to him and to you!" said Matilda. "But can I, most respected of women, can I experience all this tenderness, this world of goodness, and conceal a thought from the best of mothers?"—"What art thou going to utter?" said Isabella, trembling. "Recollect thyself, Matilda."—"No, Isabella," said the princess, "I should not deserve this incomparable parent, if the inmost recesses of my soul harboured a thought without

her permission—nay, I have offended her; I have suffered a passion to enter my heart without her avowal—but here I disclaim
it; here I vow to heaven and her"—"My child! my child!" said
Hippolita, "what words are these! what new calamities has fate in
store for us! Thou, a passion! Thou, in this hour of destruction!"
—"Oh! I see all my guilt!" said Matilda.—"I abhor myself, if I
cost my mother a pang. She is the dearest thing I have on earth—
Oh! I will never, never behold him more!"—"Isabella!" said
Hippolita, "thou art conscious to this unhappy secret; whatever
it is, speak!"—"What!" cried Matilda, "have I so forfeited my
mother's love, that she will not permit me even to speak my own
guilt? oh! wretched, wretched Matilda!"—"Thou art too cruel,"
said Isabella to Hippolita: "canst thou behold this anguish of a
virtuous mind, and not commiserate it?"—"Not pity my child!"
said Hippolita, catching Matilda in her arms—"Oh! I know she is
good, she is all virtue, all tenderness, and duty; I do forgive thee,
my excellent, my only hope!" The princesses then revealed to
Hippolita their mutual inclination for Theodore, and the purpose of Isabella to resign him to Matilda.—Hippolita blamed
their imprudence, and shewed them the improbability that either
father would consent to bestow his heiress on so poor a man,
though nobly born. Some comfort it gave her to find their passion of so recent a date, and that Theodore had but little cause
to suspect it in either. She strictly enjoined them to avoid all correspondence with him. This Matilda fervently promised; but
Isabella, who flattered herself that she meant no more than to
promote his union with her friend, could not determine to avoid
him; and made no reply. "I will go to the convent," said Hippolita, "and order new masses to be said for a deliverance from these
calamities."—"Oh! my mother," said Matilda, "you mean to quit
us: you mean to take sanctuary, and to give my father an opportunity of pursuing his fatal intention. Alas! on my knees I sup-
plicate you to forbear—will you leave me a prey to Frederic? I
will follow you to the convent."—"Be at peace, my child," said
Hippolita; "I will return instantly.—I will never abandon thee,
until I know it is the will of heaven, and for thy benefit."—"Do
not deceive me," said Matilda. "I will not marry Frederic until
thou commandest it.—Alas! what will become of me?"—"Why
that exclamation?" said Hippolita.—"I have promised thee to return."—"Ah! my mother," replied Matilda, "stay and save me

from myself. A frown from thee can do more than all my father's severity. I have given away my heart, and you alone can make me recal it."—"No more," said Hippolita; "thou must not relapse, Matilda."—"I can quit Theodore," said she, "but must I wed another? let me attend thee to the altar, and shut myself from the world for ever."—"Thy fate depends on thy father," said Hippolita; "I have ill bestowed my tenderness, if it has taught thee to revere aught beyond him. Adieu! my child: I go to pray for thee."

Hippolita's real purpose was to demand of Jerome, whether in conscience she might not consent to the divorce. She had oft urged Manfred to resign the principality, which the delicacy of her conscience rendered an hourly burden to her. These scruples concurred to make the separation from her husband appear less dreadful to her, than it would have seemed in any other situation.

Jerome, at quitting the castle over-night, had questioned Theodore severely why he had accused him to Manfred of being privy to his escape. Theodore owned it had been with the design to prevent Manfred's suspicion from alighting on Matilda; and added, the holiness of Jerome's life and character secured him from the tyrant's wrath. Jerome was heartily grieved to discover his son's inclination for that princess; and leaving him to his rest, promised in the morning to acquaint him with important reasons for conquering his passion. Theodore, like Isabella, was too recently acquainted with parental authority, to submit to its decisions against the impulse of his heart. He had little curiosity to learn the friar's reasons, and less disposition to obey them. The lovely Matilda had made stronger impressions on him than filial affection. All night he pleased himself with visions of love; and it was not till late after the morning-office, that he recollected the friar's commands to attend him at Alfonso's tomb.

"Young man," said Jerome, when he saw him, "this tardiness does not please me. Have a father's commands already so little weight?" Theodore made awkward excuses, and attributed his delay to having overslept himself. "And on whom were thy dreams employed?" said the friar, sternly. His son blushed.— "Come, come," resumed the friar, "inconsiderate youth, this must not be; eradicate this guilty passion from thy breast."—"Guilty passion!" cried Theodore, "Can guilt dwell with innocent beauty and virtuous modesty?"—"It is sinful," replied the friar, "to cherish those whom heaven has doomed to destruction. A tyrant's race must be swept from the earth to the third and fourth generation."—"Will heaven visit the innocent for the crimes of the guilty?" said Theodore. "The fair Matilda has virtues enough"—"To undo thee," interrupted Jerome. "Hast thou so soon forgotten that twice the savage Manfred has pronounced thy sentence?"—"Nor have I forgotten, sir," said Theodore, "that the charity of his daughter delivered me from his power. I can forget injuries, but never benefits."—"The injuries thou hast received from Manfred's race," said the friar, "are beyond what thou canst conceive. Reply not, but view this holy image! Beneath this marble monument rest the ashes of the good Alfonso; a prince adorned with every virtue! the father of his people! the delight of mankind! kneel, headstrong boy, and list, while a father unfolds a tale of horror, that will expel every sentiment from thy soul, but sensations of sacred vengeance.—Alfonso! much-injured prince! let thy unsatisfied shade sit awful on the troubled air, while these trembling lips—Ha! who comes there?"—"The most wretched of women!" said Hippolita, entering the choir. "Good father, art thou at leisure?—but why this kneeling youth? what means the horror imprinted on each countenance? why at this venerable tomb—alas! hast thou seen aught?"—"We were pouring forth our orisons to heaven," replied the friar, with some confusion, "to put an end to the woes of this deplorable province. Join with us, lady! thy spotless soul may obtain an exemption from the judgments which the portents of these days but too speakingly denounce against thy house."—"I pray fervently to heaven to divert them," said the pious princess. "Thou knowest it has been the occupation of my life to wrest a blessing for my lord and my harmless children—One, alas! is taken from me! would heaven but hear me for my poor Matilda! Father! intercede for her!"—"Every heart will bless her," cried Theodore, with rapture. "Be dumb, rash youth!" said Jerome. "And thou, fond princess, contend not with the powers above! the Lord giveth, and the Lord taketh away: bless his holy name, and submit to his decrees."—"I do most devoutly," said Hippolita: "but will he not spare my only comfort? must Matilda perish too? Ah! father, I came—but dismiss thy son. No ear but thine must hear what I have to utter."—"May heaven grant thy every wish, most excellent princess!" said Theodore, retiring. Jerome frowned.

Hippolita then acquainted the friar with the proposal she had suggested to Manfred, his approbation of it, and the tender of Matilda that he was gone to make to Frederic. Jerome could not conceal his dislike of the motion, which he covered under the pretence of the improbability that Frederic, the nearest of blood to Alfonso, and who was come to claim his succession, would yield to an alliance with the usurper of his right. But nothing could equal the perplexity of the friar, when Hippolita confessed her readiness not to oppose the separation, and demanded his opinion on the legality of her acquiescence. The friar catched eagerly at her request of his advice, and, without explaining his aversion to the proposed marriage of Manfred and Isabella, he painted to Hippolita, in the most alarming colours, the sinfulness of her consent, denounced judgments against her if she complied, and enjoined her, in the severest terms, to treat any such proposition with every mark of indignation and refusal.

Manfred, in the mean time, had broken his purpose to Frederic, and proposed the double marriage. That weak prince, who had been struck with the charms of Matilda, listened but too eagerly to the offer. He forgot his enmity to Manfred, whom he saw but little hope of dispossessing by force; and flattering himself that no issue might succeed from the union of his daughter with the tyrant, he looked upon his own succession to the principality as facilitated by wedding Matilda. He made faint opposition to the proposal; affecting, for form only, not to acquiesce unless Hippolita should consent to the divorce.—Manfred took that upon himself. Transported with his success, and impatient to see himself in a situation to expect sons, he hastened to his wife's apartment, determined to extort her compliance. He learned with indignation that she was absent at the convent. His guilt suggested to him that she had probably been informed by Isabella of his purpose. He doubted whether her retirement to the convent did not import an intention of remaining there, until she could raise obstacles to their divorce; and the suspicions he had already entertained of Jerome, made him apprehend that the friar would not only traverse his views, but might have inspired Hippolita with the resolution of taking sanctuary. Impatient to unravel this clue, and to defeat its success, Manfred hastened to the convent, and arrived there as the friar was earnestly exhorting the princess never to yield to the divorce.

"Madam," said Manfred, "what business drew you hither?

why did you not await my return from the marquis?"—"I came
to implore a blessing on your councils," replied Hippolita. "My
councils do not need a friar's intervention:" said Manfred—"and
of all men living is that hoary traitor the only one whom you delight to confer with?"—"Profane prince!" said Jerome; "is it at
the altar that thou choosest to insult the servants of the altar?—
but, Manfred, thy impious schemes are known. Heaven and this
virtuous lady know them—nay, frown not, prince. The church
despises thy menaces. Her thunders will be heard above thy wrath.
Dare to proceed in thy curst purpose of a divorce, until her sentence be known, and here I lance her anathema at thy head."—
"Audacious rebel!" said Manfred, endeavouring to conceal the
awe with which the friar's words inspired him; "dost thou presume to threaten thy lawful prince?"—"Thou art no lawful
prince," said Jerome; "thou art no prince—go, discuss thy claim
with Frederic: and when that is done"—"It is done," replied
Manfred; "Frederic accepts Matilda's hand, and is content to wave
his claim, unless I have no male issue"—as he spoke those words,
three drops of blood fell from the nose of Alfonso's statue. Manfred turned pale, and the princess sunk on her knees. "Behold!"
said the friar; "mark this miraculous indication that the blood of
Alfonso will never mix with that of Manfred!"—"My gracious
lord," said Hippolita, "let us submit ourselves to heaven.—Think
not thy ever obedient wife rebels against thy authority. I have no
will but that of my lord and the church. To that revered tribunal
let us appeal. It does not depend on us to burst the bonds that
unite us. If the church shall approve the dissolution of our marriage, be it so—I have but few years, and those of sorrow, to
pass. Where can they be worn away so well as at the foot of this
altar, in prayers for thine and Matilda's safety?"—"But thou shalt
not remain here until then," said Manfred. "Repair with me to
the castle, and there I will advise on the proper measures for a
divorce; but this meddling friar comes not thither: my hospitable
roof shall never more harbour a traitor—and for thy reverence's
offspring," continued he, "I banish him from my dominions. He,
I ween, is no sacred personage, nor under the protection of the
church. Whoever weds Isabella, it shall not be Father Falconara's
started-up son."—"They start up," said the friar, "who are suddenly beheld in the seat of lawful princes; but they wither away
like the grass, and their place knows them no more." Manfred,

casting a look of scorn at the friar, led Hippolita forth; but, at the door of the church, whispered one of his attendants to remain concealed about the convent, and bring him instant notice, if any one from the castle should repair thither.

CHAPTER V

Every reflection which Manfred made on the friar's behaviour, conspired to persuade him that Jerome was privy to an amour between Isabella and Theodore. But Jerome's new presumption, so dissonant from his former meekness, suggested still deeper apprehensions. The prince even suspected that the friar depended on some secret support from Frederic, whose arrival coinciding with the novel appearance of Theodore, seemed to bespeak a correspondence. Still more was he troubled with the resemblance of Theodore to Alfonso's portrait. The latter he knew had unquestionably died without issue. Frederic had consented to bestow Isabella on him.—These contradictions agitated his mind with numberless pangs. He saw but two methods of extricating himself from his difficulties. The one was to resign his dominions to the marquis—pride, ambition, and his reliance on ancient prophecies, which had pointed out a possibility of preserving them to his posterity, combated that thought. The other was to press his marriage with Isabella. After long ruminating on these anxious thoughts, as he marched silently with Hippolita to the castle, he at last discoursed with that princess on the subject of his disquiet, and used every insinuating and plausible argument to extract her consent to, even her promise of promoting the divorce. Hippolita needed little persuasion to bend her to his pleasure. She endeavoured to win him over to the measure of resigning his dominions; but, finding her exhortations fruitless, she assured him, that, as far as her conscience would allow, she would raise no opposition to a separation, though, without better-founded scruples than what he yet alleged, she would not engage to be active in demanding it.

This compliance, though inadequate, was sufficient to raise Manfred's hopes. He trusted that his power and wealth would easily advance his suit at the court of Rome, whither he resolved

to engage Frederic to take a journey on purpose. That prince had
discovered so much passion for Matilda, that Manfred hoped to
obtain all he wished, by holding out or withdrawing his daughter's charms, according as the marquis should appear more or less
disposed to co-operate in his views. Even the absence of Frederic
would be a material point gained, until he could take farther
measures for his security.

Dismissing Hippolita to her apartment, he repaired to that of
the marquis, but crossing the great hall, through which he was to
pass, he met Bianca. That damsel he knew was in the confidence
of both the young ladies. It immediately occurred to him to sift
her on the subject of Isabella and Theodore. Calling her aside into
the recess of the oriel window of the hall, and soothing her with
many fair words and promises, he demanded of her, whether she
knew aught of the state of Isabella's affections. "I! my lord! no,
my lord—yes, my lord—poor lady! she is wonderfully alarmed
about her father's wounds; but I tell her he will do well, don't
your highness think so?"—"I do not ask you," replied Manfred,
"what she thinks about her father: but you are in her secrets:
come, be a good girl, and tell me; is there any young man—ha!
you understand me."—"Lord bless me! understand your highness? no, not I: I told her a few vulnerary herbs and repose."—"I
am not talking," replied the prince, impatiently, "about her father: I know he will do well."—"Bless me, I rejoice to hear your
highness say so; for though I thought it right not to let my young
lady despond, methought his greatness had a wan look, and a
something—I remember when young Ferdinand was wounded
by the Venetian"—"Thou answerest from the point," interrupted
Manfred; "but here, take this jewel; perhaps that may fix thy attention—nay, no reverences; my favour shall not stop here—
come, tell me truly; how stands Isabella's heart?"—"Well! your
highness has such a way!" said Bianca, "to be sure—but can your
highness keep a secret?—if it should ever come out of your lips"
—"It shall not, it shall not," cried Manfred. "Nay, but swear,
your highness:—by my halidame, if it should ever be known that
I said it!—Why, truth is truth, I do not think my Lady Isabella
ever much affectioned my young lord, your son—yet he was a
sweet youth as one should see—I am sure, if I had been a princess
—but bless me! I must attend my Lady Matilda; she will marvel
what is become of me."—"Stay," cried Manfred; "thou hast not

satisfied my question. Hast thou ever carried any message, any letter?"—"I! good gracious!" cried Bianca; "I carry a letter? I would not, to be a queen. I hope your highness thinks, though I am poor, I am honest;—did your highness never hear what Count Marsigli offered me, when he came a wooing to my Lady Matilda?"—"I have not leisure," said Manfred, "to listen to thy tales. I do not question thy honesty; but it is thy duty to conceal nothing from me. How long has Isabella been acquainted with Theodore?"—"Nay, there is nothing can escape your highness!" said Bianca—"not that I know anything of the matter—Theodore, to be sure, is a proper young man, and, as my Lady Matilda says, the very image of good Alfonso: has not your highness remarked it?" —"Yes, yes,—No—thou torturest me," said Manfred. "Where did they meet?—when?"—"Who! my Lady Matilda?" said Bianca. "No, no, not Matilda; Isabella. When did Isabella first become acquainted with this Theodore?"—"Virgin Mary!" said Bianca, "how should I know?"—"Thou dost know," said Manfred, "and I must know; I will."—"Lord! your highness is not jealous of young Theodore!" said Bianca. "Jealous! no, no: why should I be jealous?—perhaps I mean to unite them. If I were sure Isabella would have no repugnance"—"Repugnance! no, I'll warrant her," said Bianca: "he is as comely a youth as ever trod on Christian ground. We are all in love with him; there is not a soul in the castle but would be rejoiced to have him for our prince—I mean, when it shall please Heaven to call your highness to itself." —"Indeed!" said Manfred; "has it gone so far! oh! this cursed friar!—but I must not lose time:—go, Bianca, attend Isabella; but, I charge thee, not a word of what has passed. Find out how she is affected towards Theodore: bring me good news, and that ring has a companion. Wait at the foot of the winding staircase: I am going to visit the marquis, and will talk farther with thee at my return."

Manfred, after some general conversation, desired Frederic to dismiss the two knights, his companions, having to talk with him on urgent affairs. As soon as they were alone, he began, in artful guise, to sound the marquis on the subject of Matilda; and, finding him disposed to his wish, he let drop hints on the difficulties that would attend the celebration of their marriage, unless—at that instant Bianca burst into the room, with a wildness in her look and gestures that spoke the utmost terror. "Oh! my lord, my lord!" cried she, "we are all undone! it is come again! it is come again!"—"What is come again?" cried Manfred, amazed. "Oh! the hand! the giant! the hand!—support me! I am terrified out of my senses," cried Bianca. "I will not sleep in the castle to-night. Where shall I go?—my things may come after me to-morrow— would I had been content to wed Francisco!—this comes of am- bition!"—"What has terrified thee thus, young woman?" said the marquis; "thou art safe here; be not alarmed."—"Oh! your great- ness is wonderfully good," said Bianca, "but I dare not—no, pray let me go—I had rather leave everything behind me, than stay another hour under this roof."—"Go to—thou hast lost thy senses," said Manfred. "Interrupt us not; we were communing on important matters. My lord, this wench is subject to fits. Come with me, Bianca."—"Oh! the saints! no," said Bianca; "for cer- tain it comes to warn your highness: why should it appear to me else? I say my prayers morning and evening—oh! if your highness had believed Diego! 'tis the same hand that he saw the foot to in the gallery-chamber—Father Jerome has often told us the prophecy would be out one of these days. 'Bianca,' said he, 'mark my words' "—"Thou ravest," said Manfred, in a rage; "be gone, and keep these fooleries to frighten thy companions."—"What! my lord," cried Bianca, "do you think I have seen nothing? go to the foot of the great stairs yourself—as I live, I saw it."—"Saw what? tell us, fair maid, what thou hast seen," said Frederic. "Can your highness listen," said Manfred, "to the delirium of a silly wench, who has heard stories of apparitions until she believes them?"—"This is more than fancy," said the marquis; "her terror is too natural, and too strongly impressed, to be the work of imag- ination. Tell us, fair maiden, what it is has moved thee thus."— "Yes, my lord; thank your greatness," said Bianca; "I believe I look very pale; I shall be better when I have recovered myself. I was going to my Lady Isabella's chamber, by his highness's or- der"—"We do not want the circumstances," interrupted Man- fred: "since his highness will have it so, proceed; but be brief." —"Lord! your highness thwarts one so!" replied Bianca: "I fear my hair—I am sure I never in my life—well! as I was telling your greatness, I was going, by his highness's order, to my Lady Isa- bella's chamber: she lies in the watchet-coloured chamber, on the right hand, one pair of stairs: so when I came to the great stairs, I was looking on his highness's present here"—"Grant me patience," said Manfred: "will this wench never come to the point? what imports it to the marquis, that I gave thee a bauble for thy faithful attendance on my daughter? we want to know what thou sawest."—"I was going to tell your highness," said Bianca, "if you would permit me.—So as I was rubbing the ring—I am sure I had not gone up three steps, but I heard the rattling of armour; for all the world such a clatter, as Diego says he heard when the giant turned him about in the gallery-chamber."— "What does she mean, my lord!" said the marquis: "is your castle haunted by giants and goblins?" "Lord! what, has not your greatness heard the story of the giant in the gallery-chamber?" cried Bianca. "I marvel his highness has not told you—mayhap you do not know there is a prophecy"—"This trifling is intolerable," interrupted Manfred. "Let us dismiss this silly wench, my lord! we have more important affairs to discuss."—"By your favour," said Frederic, "these are no trifles: the enormous sabre I was directed to in the wood, yon casque, its fellow—are these visions of this poor maiden's brain?"—"So Jaquez thinks, may it please your greatness," said Bianca. "He says this moon will not be out without our seeing some strange revolution. For my part I should not be surprised if it was to happen to-morrow; for, as I was saying, when I heard the clattering of armour, I was all in a cold sweat— I looked up, and if your greatness will believe me, I saw upon the uppermost bannister of the great stairs a hand in armour as big, as big—I thought I should have swooned—I never stopped until I came hither—would I were well out of this castle! My Lady Matilda told me but yester-morning that her highness Hippolita knows something"—"Thou art an insolent!" cried Manfred.— "Lord Marquis, it much misgives me that this scene is concerted to affront me. Are my own domestics suborned to spread tales injurious to my honour? Pursue your claim by manly daring; or let us bury our feuds, as was proposed, by the intermarriage of our children: but trust me, it ill becomes a prince of your bearing to practise on mercenary wenches."—"I scorn your imputation," said Frederic; "until this hour I never set eyes on this damsel: I have given her no jewel! my lord, my lord, your conscience, your guilt accuses you, and you would throw the suspicion on me— but keep your daughter, and think no more of Isabella: the judgments already fallen on your house forbid me matching into it."

Manfred, alarmed at the resolute tone in which Frederic delivered these words, endeavoured to pacify him. Dismissing Bianca, he made such submissions to the marquis, and threw in such artful encomiums on Matilda, that Frederic was once more staggered. However, as his passion was of so recent a date, it could not, at once, surmount the scruples he had conceived. He had gathered enough from Bianca's discourse to persuade him that Heaven declared itself against Manfred. The proposed marriages too removed his claim to a distance; and the principality of Otranto was a stronger temptation, than the contingent reversion of it with Matilda. Still he would not absolutely recede from his engagements; but purposing to gain time, he demanded of Manfred if it was true in fact that Hippolita consented to the divorce. The prince, transported to find no other obstacle, and depending on his influence over his wife, assured the marquis it was so, and that he might satisfy himself of the truth from her own mouth.

As they were thus discoursing, word was brought that the banquet was prepared. Manfred conducted Frederic to the great hall, where they were received by Hippolita and the young princesses. Manfred placed the marquis next to Matilda, and seated himself between his wife and Isabella. Hippolita comported herself with an easy gravity; but the young ladies were silent and melancholy. Manfred, who was determined to pursue his point with the marquis in the remainder of the evening, pushed on the feast until it waxed late; affecting unrestrained gaiety, and plying Frederic with repeated goblets of wine. The latter, more upon his guard than Manfred wished, declined his frequent challenges, on pretence of his late loss of blood; while the prince, to raise his own disordered spirits, and to counterfeit unconcern, indulged himself in plentiful draughts, though not to the intoxication of his senses.

The evening being far advanced, the banquet concluded. Manfred would have withdrawn with Frederic; but the latter pleading weakness, and want of repose, retired to his chamber, gallantly telling the prince, that his daughter should amuse his highness until himself could attend him. Manfred accepted the party, and, to the no small grief of Isabella, accompanied her to her apartment. Matilda waited on her mother to enjoy the freshness of the evening on the ramparts of the castle.

Soon as the company were dispersed their several ways, Frederic, quitting his chamber, inquired if Hippolita was alone, and was told by one of her attendants, who had not noticed her going forth, that, at that hour, she generally withdrew to her oratory, where he probably would find her. The marquis, during the repast, had beheld Matilda with increase of passion. He now wished to find Hippolita in the disposition her lord had promised. The portents that had alarmed him were forgotten in his desires. Stealing softly and unobserved to the apartment of Hippolita, he entered it with a resolution to encourage her acquiescence to the divorce, having perceived that Manfred was resolved to make the possession of Isabella an unalterable condition, before he would grant Matilda to his wishes.

The marquis was not surprised at the silence that reigned in the princess's apartment. Concluding her, as he had been advertised, in her oratory, he passed on. The door was ajar; the evening gloomy and overcast. Pushing open the door gently, he saw a person kneeling before the altar. As he approached nearer, it seemed not a woman, but one in a long woollen weed, whose back was towards him. The person seemed absorbed in prayer. The marquis was about to return, when the figure, rising, stood some moments fixed in meditation, without regarding him. The marquis, expecting the holy person to come forth, and meaning to excuse his uncivil interruption, said, "Reverend father, I sought the Lady Hippolita."—"Hippolita!" replied a hollow voice, "camest thou to this castle to seek Hippolita?" and then the figure, turning slowly round, discovered to Frederic the fleshless jaws and empty sockets of a skeleton, wrapt in a hermit's cowl. "Angels of grace, protect me!" cried Frederic, recoiling. "Deserve their protection!" said the spectre. Frederic, falling on his knees, adjured the phantom to take pity on him. "Dost thou not remember me?" said the apparition: "Remember the wood of Joppa!"—"Art thou that holy hermit?" cried Frederic, trembling; "Can I do aught for thy eternal peace?"—"Wast thou delivered from bondage," said the spectre, "to pursue carnal delights?—Hast thou forgotten the buried sabre, and the behest of heaven engraven on it?"—"I have not, I have not," said Frederic; "but say, blest spirit, what is thy errand to me?—what remains to be done?"—"To forget Matilda!" said the apparition—and vanished.

Frederic's blood froze in his veins. For some minutes he remained motionless. Then, falling prostrate on his face before the altar, he besought the intercession of every saint for pardon. A flood of tears succeeded to this transport; and the image of the beauteous Matilda, rushing, in spite of him, on his thoughts, he lay on the ground in a conflict of penitence and passion. Ere he could recover from this agony of his spirits, the Princess Hippolita, with a taper in her hand, entered the oratory alone. Seeing a man, without motion, on the floor, she gave a shriek, concluding him dead. Her fright brought Frederic to himself. Rising suddenly, his face bedewed with tears, he would have rushed from her presence; but Hippolita, stopping him, conjured him, in the most plaintive accents, to explain the cause of his disorder, and by what strange chance she had found him there in that posture. "Ah! virtuous princess," said the marquis, penetrated with grief—and stopped. "For the love of Heaven, my lord," said Hippolita, "disclose the cause of this transport! what mean these doleful sounds, this alarming exclamation on my name? What woes has Heaven still in store for the wretched Hippolita?—Yet silent!—By every pitying angel, I adjure thee, noble prince," continued she, falling at his feet, "to disclose the purport of what lies at thy heart—I see thou feelest for me; thou feelest the sharp pangs that thou inflictest—speak, for pity!—does aught thou knowest concern my child?"—"I cannot speak," cried Frederic, bursting from her —"Oh! Matilda!"

Quitting the princess thus abruptly, he hastened to his own apartment. At the door of it he was accosted by Manfred, who, flushed by wine and love, had come to seek him, and to propose to waste some hours of the night in music and revelling. Frederic, offended at an invitation so dissonant from the mood of his soul, pushed him rudely aside, and, entering his chamber, flung the door intemperately against Manfred, and bolted it inwards. The haughty prince, enraged at this unaccountable behaviour, withdrew in a frame of mind capable of the most fatal excesses. As he crossed the court, he was met by the domestic whom he had planted at the convent, as a spy on Jerome and Theodore. This man, almost breathless with the haste he had made, informed his lord, that Theodore and some lady from the castle, were, at that instant, in private conference at the tomb of Alfonso, in St. Nicholas's church. He had dogged Theodore thither, but the gloominess of the night had prevented his discovering who the woman was.

Manfred, whose spirits were inflamed, and whom Isabella had driven from her on his urging his passion with too little reserve, did not doubt but the inquietude she had expressed had been occasioned by her impatience to meet Theodore. Provoked by this conjecture, and enraged at her father, he hastened secretly to the great church. Gliding softly between the aisles, and guided by an imperfect gleam of moonshine that shone faintly through the illuminated windows, he stole towards the tomb of Alfonso, to which he was directed by indistinct whispers of the persons he sought.—The first sounds he could distinguish were—"Does it, alas! depend on me? Manfred will never permit our union."—"No, this shall prevent it!" cried the tyrant, drawing his dagger, and plunging it over her shoulder into the bosom of the person that spoke—"Ah, me! I am slain!" cried Matilda, sinking; "good Heaven, receive my soul!"—"Savage, inhuman monster! what hast thou done?" cried Theodore, rushing on him, and wrenching his dagger from him—"Stop, stop thy impious hand!" cried Matilda: "it is my father!" Manfred, waking as from a trance, beat his breast, twisted his hands in his locks, and endeavoured to recover his dagger from Theodore, to dispatch himself. Theodore, scarce less distracted, and only mastering the transports of his grief to assist Matilda, had now, by his cries, drawn some of the monks to his aid. While part of them endeavoured, in concert with the afflicted Theodore, to stop the blood of the dying princess, the rest prevented Manfred from laying violent hands on himself.

Matilda, resigning herself patiently to her fate, acknowledged, with looks of grateful love, the zeal of Theodore. Yet, oft as her faintness would permit her speech its way, she begged the assistants to comfort her father. Jerome, by this time, had learnt the fatal news, and reached the church. His looks seemed to reproach Theodore: but, turning to Manfred, he said, "Now, tyrant! behold the completion of woe fulfilled on thy impious and devoted head! The blood of Alfonso cried to Heaven for vengeance, and Heaven has permitted its altar to be polluted by assassination, that thou mightest shed thy own blood at the foot of that prince's sepulchre!"—"Cruel man!" cried Matilda, "to aggravate the woes of a parent! may Heaven bless my father, and forgive him as I do! My lord, my gracious sire, dost thou forgive thy child? Indeed, I came not hither to meet Theodore! I found him praying at this tomb, whither my mother sent me to intercede for thee, for her—dearest father, bless your child, and say you forgive her."—"Forgive thee! murderous monster!" cried Manfred—"can assassins forgive! I took thee for Isabella; but Heaven directed my bloody hand to the heart of my child—oh! Matilda—I cannot utter it—canst thou forgive the blindness of my rage?"—"I can, I do! and may Heaven confirm it!" said Matilda—"but, while I have life to ask it—Oh! my mother! what will she feel!—will you comfort her, my lord; will you not put her away? indeed she loves you—oh! I am faint! bear me to the castle—can I live to have her close my eyes?"

Theodore and the monks besought her earnestly to suffer herself to be borne into the convent; but her instances were so pressing to be carried to the castle, that, placing her on a litter, they conveyed her thither as she requested; Theodore supporting her head with his arm, and hanging over her in an agony of despairing love, still endeavoured to inspire her with hopes of life. Jerome, on the other side, comforted her with discourses of Heaven, and, holding a crucifix before her, which she bathed with innocent tears, prepared her for her passage to immortality. Manfred, plunged in the deepest affliction, followed the litter in despair.

Ere they reached the castle, Hippolita, informed of the dreadful catastrophe, had flown to meet her murdered child: but when she saw the afflicted procession, the mightiness of her grief deprived her of her senses, and she fell lifeless to the earth in a swoon. Isabella and Frederic, who attended her, were overwhelmed in almost equal sorrow. Matilda alone seemed insensible to her own situation: every thought was lost in tenderness for her mother. Ordering the litter to stop, as soon as Hippolita was brought to herself, she asked for her father. He approached, unable to speak. Matilda, seizing his hand and her mother's, locked them in her own, and then clasped them to her heart. Manfred could not support this act of pathetic piety. He dashed himself on the ground, and cursed the day he was born. Isabella, apprehensive that these struggles of passion were more than Matilda could support, took upon herself to order Manfred to be borne to his apartment, while she caused Matilda to be conveyed to the nearest chamber. Hippolita, scarce more alive than her daughter, was regardless of everything but her: but when the tender Isabella's care would have likewise removed her, while the surgeons examined Matilda's wound, she cried, "Remove me! never! never! I lived but in her, and will expire with her." Matilda raised her eyes, at her mother's voice, but closed them again without speaking. Her sinking pulse, and the damp coldness of her hand, soon dispelled all hopes of recovery. Theodore followed the surgeons into the outer chamber, and heard them pronounce the fatal sentence, with a transport equal to frenzy—"Since she cannot live mine," cried he, "at least she shall be mine in death! Father! Jerome! will you not join our hands!" cried he to the friar, who, with the marquis, had accompanied the surgeons. "What means thy distracted rashness?" said Jerome: "Is this an hour for marriage?"—"It is, it is," cried Theodore; "alas! there is no other!"—"Young man, thou art too unadvised," said Frederic:—"Dost thou think we are to listen to thy fond transports in this hour of fate?—what pretensions hast thou to the princess?"—"Those of a prince," said Theodore—"of the sovereign of Otranto. This reverend man, my father, has informed me who I am."—"Thou ravest," said the marquis: "there is no Prince of Otranto but myself, now Manfred, by murder, by sacrilegious murder, has forfeited all pretensions."—"My lord," said Jerome, assuming an air of command, "he tells you true. It was not my purpose the secret should have been divulged so soon; but fate presses onward to its work. What his hot-headed passion has revealed, my tongue confirms. Know, prince, that when Alfonso set sail for the Holy Land"—"Is this a season for explanations?" cried Theodore:—"Father, come and unite me to the princess; she shall be mine—in every other thing I will dutifully obey you. My life, my adored Matilda!" continued Theodore, rushing back into the inner chamber, "will you not be mine? will you not bless your"—Isabella made signs to him to be silent, apprehending the princess was near her end. "What! is she dead?" cried Theodore: "is it possible!"—The violence of his exclamations brought Matilda to herself. Lifting up her eyes, she looked round for her mother—"Life of my soul! I am here," cried Hippolita; "think not I will quit thee!"—"Oh! you are too good," said Matilda—"but weep not for me, my mother! I am going where sorrow never dwells—Isabella, thou hast loved me; wo't thou not supply my fondness to this dear, dear woman?—indeed I am faint!"—"Oh! my child! my child!" said Hippolita, in a flood of tears; "can I not withhold thee a moment?"—"It will not be," said Matilda—"commend me to Heaven:—where is my father?—forgive him, dearest mother—forgive him my death; it was an error—Oh! I had forgotten—dearest mother, I vowed never to see

Theodore more—perhaps that has drawn down this calamity—
but it was not intentional—can you pardon me?"—"Oh! wound
not my agonizing soul!" said Hippolita; "thou never could'st offend me—Alas! she faints! help! help!"—"I would say something
more," said Matilda, struggling; "but it wonnot be—Isabella—
Theodore—for my sake—Oh!"—she expired. Isabella and her
women tore Hippolita from the corse; but Theodore threatened
destruction to all who attempted to remove him from it. He
printed a thousand kisses on her clay-cold hands, and uttered
every expression that despairing love could dictate.

Isabella, in the mean time, was accompanying the afflicted
Hippolita to her apartment; but, in the middle of the court, they
were met by Manfred, who, distracted with his own thoughts,
and anxious once more to behold his daughter, was advancing to
the chamber where she lay. As the moon was now at its height, he
read in the countenances of this unhappy company, the event he
dreaded. "What? is she dead?" cried he, in wild confusion—a
clap of thunder, at that instant, shook the castle to its foundations; the earth rocked, and the clank of more than mortal armour was heard behind. Frederic and Jerome thought the last
day was at hand. The latter, forcing Theodore along with them,
rushed into the court. The moment Theodore appeared, the walls
of the castle behind Manfred were thrown down with a mighty
force, and the form of Alfonso, dilated to an immense magnitude,
appeared in the centre of the ruins. "Behold in Theodore the true
heir of Alfonso!" said the vision: and having pronounced these
words, accompanied by a clap of thunder, it ascended solemnly
towards Heaven, where, the clouds parting asunder, the form of
St. Nicholas was seen, and, receiving Alfonso's shade, they were
soon wrapt from mortal eyes in a blaze of glory.

The beholders fell prostrate on their faces, acknowledging the
divine will. The first that broke silence was Hippolita. "My lord,"
said she, to the desponding Manfred, "behold the vanity of human greatness! Conrad is gone! Matilda is no more! in Theodore
we view the true Prince of Otranto. By what miracle he is so, I
know not—suffice it to us, our doom is pronounced! shall we not,
—can we do other than dedicate the few deplorable hours we
have to live, in deprecating the farther wrath of heaven? Heaven
ejects us—whither can we fly, but to yon holy cells that yet offer
us a retreat?"—"Thou guiltless, but unhappy woman! unhappy

by my crimes!" replied Manfred, "my heart, at last, is open to thy devout admonitions. Oh! could—but it cannot be—ye are lost in wonder—let me at last do justice on myself! To heap shame on my own head is all the satisfaction I have left to offer to offended Heaven. My story has drawn down these judgments: let my confession atone—but ah! what can atone for usurpation, and a murdered child! a child murdered in a consecrated place!—List, sirs, and may this bloody record be a warning to future tyrants!

"Alfonso, ye all know, died in the Holy Land—ye would interrupt me; ye would say he came not fairly to his end—it is most true—why else this bitter cup which Manfred must drink to the dregs? Ricardo, my grandfather, was his chamberlain—I would draw a veil over my ancestor's crimes—but it is in vain! Alfonso died by poison. A fictitious will declared Ricardo his heir. His crimes pursued him—yet he lost no Conrad, no Matilda! I pay the price of usurpation for all! A storm overtook him. Haunted by his guilt, he vowed to St. Nicholas to found a church and two convents, if he lived to reach Otranto. The sacrifice was accepted: the saint appeared to him in a dream, and promised that Ricardo's posterity should reign in Otranto, until the rightful owner should be grown too large to inhabit the castle, and as long as issue male from Ricardo's loins should remain to enjoy it—Alas! alas! nor male nor female, except myself, remains of all his wretched race!—I have done—the woes of these three days speak the rest. How this young man can be Alfonso's heir, I know not —yet I do not doubt it. His are these dominions; I resign them— yet I knew not Alfonso had an heir—I question not the will of Heaven—poverty and prayer must fill up the woeful space until Manfred shall be summoned to Ricardo."

"What remains, is my part to declare," said Jerome. "When Alfonso set sail for the Holy Land, he was driven by a storm on the coast of Sicily. The other vessel, which bore Ricardo and his train, as your lordship must have heard, was separated from him."—"It is most true," said Manfred; "and the title you give me is more than an outcast can claim—well! be it so—proceed." Jerome blushed, and continued. "For three months, Lord Alfonso was wind-bound in Sicily. There he became enamoured of a fair virgin, named Victoria. He was too pious to tempt her to forbidden pleasures. They were married.—Yet, deeming this amour incongruous with the holy vow of arms by which he was bound, he

determined to conceal their nuptials, until his return from the
Crusade, when he purposed to seek and acknowledge her for his
lawful wife. He left her pregnant. During his absence, she was
delivered of a daughter: but scarce had she felt a mother's pangs,
ere she heard the fatal rumour of her lord's death, and the succession of Ricardo. What could a friendless, helpless woman do?
Would her testimony avail?—yet, my lord, I have an authentic
writing"—"It needs not," said Manfred; "the horrors of these
days, the vision we have but now seen, all corroborate thy evidence beyond a thousand parchments. Matilda's death, and my
expulsion"—"Be composed, my lord," said Hippolita; "this holy
man did not mean to recal your griefs." Jerome proceeded.

"I shall not dwell on what is needless.—The daughter of which
Victoria was delivered, was, at her maturity, bestowed in marriage
on me. Victoria died; and the secret remained locked in my
breast. Theodore's narrative has told the rest."

The friar ceased. The disconsolate company retired to the remaining part of the castle. In the morning, Manfred signed his
abdication of the principality, with the approbation of Hippolita, and each took on them the habit of religion, in the neighbouring convents. Frederic offered his daughter to the new prince,
which Hippolita's tenderness for Isabella concurred to promote:
but Theodore's grief was too fresh to admit the thought of another
love; and it was not until after frequent discourses with Isabella
of his dear Matilda, that he was persuaded he could know no
happiness but in the society of one, with whom he could for ever
indulge the melancholy that had taken possession of his soul.